The Children of Eden

SHAIDA ESCOFFERY

ISBN: 069236076X
ISBN-13: 978-0692360767

DEDICATION

To my parents: Your marriage, your love for God, and your unwavering support, inspires me everyday. I love you

THE FAMILY TREE

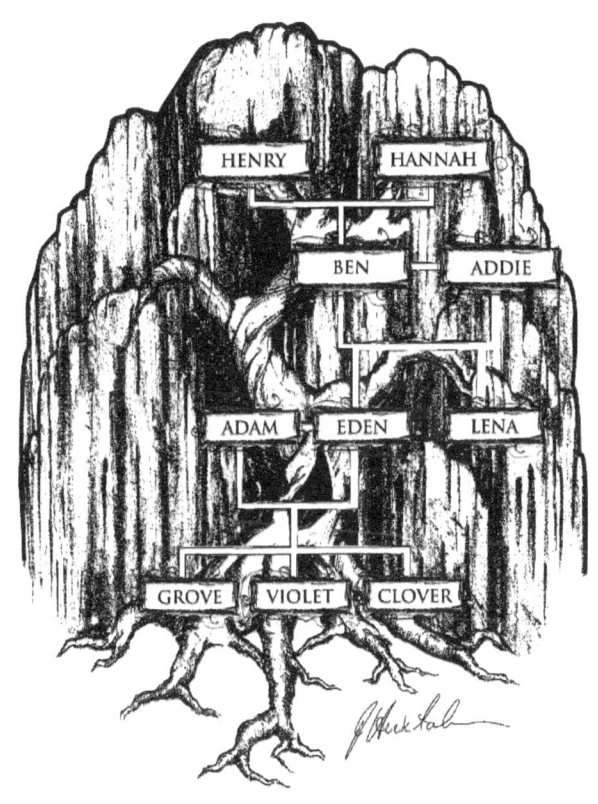

ACKNOWLEDGMENTS

Every time I'm able to complete another novel I breathe a word of thanks to God. I seriously would not be able to do these books without him!

Again, a special thanks to my parents, and to my brother for being my support system. Love you all with everything in me. To my extended family in NYC, thank you all so much for being there for me while I juggled writing and going to grad school at the same time.

To my friends, Timothy, Darian, Mikaela, Kayla, Atara, Eboni, and Raven, thank you guys for keeping laughter in my life while I went through such a huge transition in my life. You all let me vent, talk about my ideas for the book, and just be my usual goofy self. I love you guys.

To my church family, thanks for everything. Your support and prayers mean the world to me.

Thank you Stephen McCarthy for your amazing cover designs, you did it again! Thank you Kayla Lott for the ads you work so diligently on. You're the best! Also, thank you Rudy's Production Studios for your amazing photos! I finally look like a grown woman!

To my readers, every time I thought about quitting, you all kept me going. Each day I felt overwhelmed with writing and being a full time student, I remembered that it's not about me! You all motivate me everyday to keep writing. This book would've definitely not been able to happen without the motivation and support from my readers. Thank you!

CLOVER

We've been going to Idlewild ever since I can remember. Every summer, no matter what. I couldn't use my dance classes as an excuse, or my friends as an excuse. We were going and that was that. End of discussion.

It wasn't that I didn't like Idlewild, it was just that it was so quiet and there wasn't a whole lot to do once you swam, got ice cream and caught fireflies. After that, the days just seemed to go by slowly.

When I was nine, my brother Grove, my twin sister Violet, and I decided to go exploring. Well, actually Grove told us that the blue house which belonged to our dead grandparents was haunted, and of course egged us on to go inside. Violet and I couldn't act like we were scared, so we told our parents we were going outside to play. We rode our bikes over to the blue house. I remember feeling an extra chill in the air, other than the normal Michigan summer weather. I focused on the trees that lined the streets, the sound of the leaves whispering as the breeze touched them. The trees here were different from the ones back home in Miami. Of course they looked different, but I thought of the trees as different types of dancers. I think palm trees are contemporary dancers, they bend.

The house was in good condition, we all knew that my parents and grandparents made sure the house was in good condition. Every two to three weeks they'd come by and dust and clean. Mom never took us when she went. So that's why when we were kids all of us knew about this house from stories but hadn't stepped foot inside.

"How are we supposed to get inside?" Violet said, as we parked our bikes.

Grove took a pair of keys out of his pocket.

"Where'd you get that?" I asked.

"Took it from home. I'll put it back once we get inside."

"OOOOOHHHH!!" Violet said, "You took those keys." She shook her head. "Now we're gonna get in trouble. I'm going back home."

"No, we're not. You're not going to tell, are you?" Grove asked.

Violet rolled her eyes. "No," she muttered.

"Ok, so we're going inside."

When you're scared, everything seems to be happening in slow motion, you can feel your heart beat in your chest, in your ears, everywhere. The sound of the lock as Grove turned the key was magnified. When he finally got the door open, Violet held out her hand for me. "Are you coming?"

I nodded and we stepped inside. It didn't seem as creepy as Grove made it out to be. There weren't even any cobwebs. Inside was just beige with all these green accents. Spring leaf green pillows, curtains, blankets. My favorite color.

I looked to see pictures on the walls. Lots of pictures. Some were old and brown and some were newer. I released my sister's hand and walked up to the wall where an aged picture of a woman and man smiling as they held hands and walked down a road. I recognized it. My mom had shown us this picture.

"That's grandma and grandpa, right?" Violet asked.

"Yeah," I said, still looking at the picture.

"Grandma was really pretty." Violet said.

"Grandpa looks cuter than Jett Jackson, well if his pants weren't past his belly button," I said.

Grove rolled his eyes. "This is why I want a brother," he muttered.

We turned away from the picture and Grove walked towards the stairs with a rose design. "I was reading Goosebumps yesterday, 'Escape from Horror House'-"

"Grove, we don't want to hear anymore spooky stuff," I said.

He smiled slyly and then jumped at us. "Boo!"

Violet and I screamed. Violet smacked him. "Stop!"

"Ok, I'm just messing with you guys," he said with a boyish grin. My brother was the only one with my mother's eyes. They were almost the color of pennies.

"So, it's not haunted?" I said.

"No," he said.

Violet sighed from relief. I spotted a box over in the corner. I went over and pulled out a paper cover that said, "Dooley Wilson: As Time Goes By". A big black giant CD was inside.

"What's this?"

"A record," Grove said.

"How do you know?" Violet said.

"Duh, I read."

Grove was a walking encyclopedia. Grove is still a walking encyclopedia. His favorite room in our house in Idlewild was the old fashioned library that reminded me of a scaled down version of the library in *Beauty and the Beast*.

"Does it play music?" I asked.

"Yes."

"How?" Violet said.

"You need a record player."

"How are we supposed to get one of those?" I asked.

"Oh, I think Grandma has one of those!"

"Let's go," I said. The only thing on my mind was that I wanted to play this so I could dance to it. But, when we got to our grandparent's house, Grandma gave all of us a lecture on stealing and going places without permission. Then she tapped Grandpa and he stepped in the ring telling us how we could get spankings, lose our parents trust, or worse if our behavior continued, we could go to jail.

When they were done talking for what seemed like an eternity, Grandpa smiled at us and then put the record on and I heard the jazzy voice of a man fill the air.

Grandpa held out his hand for me. "Come on sweet pea. I know your itching to learn some new moves."

After that day I asked for all the records in the house and for my own record player. I started asking my mom questions about my grandma and grandpa. I just loved hearing stories about them, picturing the people in the photos I saw in the house.

They had to be fascinating people to own these records. To have traveled to Paris and found love.

I think learning about my grandparents made me fall in love with the idea of love. Ballet made me think of love.

Violet and I used to stay up and talk about how life would be once we met the love of our lives. The funny thing is that Violet always paid more attention than me even if she seemed like she wasn't. Cause while I was only paying attention to the picture that was on the wall that day and idealizing the day I would walk hand and hand with someone, Violet was reading the inscription underneath. *"Aimer, ce n'est pas se regarder l'un l'autre, c'est regarder ensemble dans la même direction."* Love does not consist in looking at each other, but rather in, together, looking in the same direction.

My mom taught us all French. Her dad taught her, and my great grandma taught him. She would always talk about connecting back to our family history and passing things on.

I rolled over in bed, wrapping myself in my comforter. Staying warm was still a priority in March in Manhattan. Especially when you're from Florida. I had already grown to hate the terms polar vortex, cold front, and freezing rain...and let's not forget snow and blizzard.

My roommate, Arya, came barging through the door. "Are you going to the studio today?"

"Not sure," I said.

"I think you're just trying to avoid Keith."

I rolled my eyes. "Keith is persistent. But there's no...connection. Come on, he's one of the business types from Stern. What are we going to talk about? Taxes?"

"'It wouldn't hurt since you have no idea how to do them...not to mention you suck at math. 'Connections' haven't worked for you. All they've done is make you a bitter woman. You know, I need to bring my Indian mother here. She would tell you compatibility first, connection after."

"That doesn't sound very romantic."

Arya laughed, "You sound like an American," she said, imitating her mother.

"I am an American college junior who needs a little romance in my life."

Arya rolled her eyes and smirked. She got up and headed to the bathroom, but turned around, "Oh hey, I got your mail," she said, tossing me a thick, large envelope.

I stared at the postage stamp. "From Eden Davis? Is this a joke?" I said out loud.

"What's wrong?"

"Eden Davis is my mother."

"I thought you said your mother passed."

"She did."

TO: CLOVER

Legacy. I think that's the word everyone secretly lives for even though they can't put it into words. They chase after money so that they can be known as the richest person in the US or maybe even the world. They want to leave it to their kids to carry on the family business. Or maybe others do tons of charity work so that when they die someone will remember their name. Remember their face, remember what they did. We all live for legacy, even if we don't say it. It's the only thing after death that really means anything. I mean the kids or grandkids can squander the money, can forget about the missions trips you did, but your legacy is yours. Kids will make a separate legacy for themselves.

It's been a year since my death. A year since I've seen you all. I've asked your father to send you this a year after. I would hope that everything will be ok in your life, but I know there must be this missing piece even while you are away at school. With Grove in grad school, Violet at RISD, I know being alone at NYU must be tough. I'm sorry I couldn't be there for your senior recitals.

I know none of us were expecting me to go so soon. It certainly wasn't what I planned on, dying soon after we'd gotten an empty nest. I was looking forward to spending time with your father, to seeing my grandkids.

Last spring when all the flowers began to bloom, life was coming back into the world, but at the same time life was being sucked from it. I suppose I'm the person that proves that you can be the healthiest person and still have unexpected things happen to you.

I didn't think anything was wrong until I

started forgetting things. Mixing up your birthdays, forgetting that you were the twin with the birthmark on your back, and Violet was the one with the shellfish allergy. I knew that, but yet there were moments I just couldn't remember the simplest things. I'd have to write it down. I tried to hide it from you guys and sometimes I regret that. That I told you by the time it was nearly over. I know Violet and Grove were angry about that. I just didn't want you all to worry while you had to deal with school.

Lupus. The name even sounds a bit evil, don't you think? You see, according to what they explained to me, it's an autoimmune disease where your body suddenly has amnesia and doesn't know if your own cells are foreign or not. It's the worst example of friendly fire. Your body betrays you and attacks itself. Me, well, my lungs were under attack and so was my brain. It's sort of strange, because according to the doctors, most people have to deal with kidney problems, which would've been a no brainer because I'm pretty sure your father would've ripped out his kidney to save me.

I don't mean to rehash all the ugly details of my sickness. I guess I'm just rambling. Maybe it's a side effect. I decided to write these to you because I don't know how much longer I have to explain things to you all. To leave with you all different parts of my life. Each of you won't get the complete story, you'll have to find each other for the next portions.

I want you to know I'm not afraid of dying. I know where I'll be. I know I won't have anymore pain in my lungs or forgetfulness. I know I won't have to be fed, or have someone bathe me. I won't be a vegetable in heaven. My only hope for here is that my husband and children will continue to live and not let my death be theirs as well.

Your father and I talked to you about many things. We tried to leave so many things with you all: A love for people, a value for education, and a trust in God. There was a legacy I wanted to leave with you all. Stories I wanted to tell you all once *you were ready. But, I hope after reading this you will see it's not just the story of Eden Davis or Adam Davis, but the story of us all.*

Remember when I taught you and Violet how to do chaine turns? While Violet was dizzily crashing into the furniture. you were just turning across the rug, spotting, with almost perfect arm structure, all on your first try. You were a natural.

This portion of the story goes to you because you need this part the most. I was a girl just like you a while back, looking out over Lake Idlewild wondering if this was all my life would be. I'd seen the lights and the excitement of the city on TV. My parents and I had gone to Chicago and to Detroit a couple times and I loved it.

Your Aunt Lena and I always used to talk about moving off to the city. Lena always said she'd go to Chicago while I was open to other possibilities.

"I can't be a professional dancer in Idlewild."

"There used to be some here."

"Yeah, a long time ago."

We shared a room upstairs, our twin sized beds across from one another. As you know, sharing a room with your sister can be one of the best things, and one of the most annoying things. We fought over what color to paint the walls, Lena wanted pink, I wanted yellow. My mom had regulated the fight by painting the side of the wall where Lena slept pink, and the side I was on, yellow. We borrowed one another's clothes and fought over things not getting returned. But each night, we lay there talking about our dreams, our parents, school... Now that I think about it, it didn't matter what we talked about. It mattered that we talked.

"What if one of us meets a guy here?" Lena asked.

"You're always talking about that. Guys don't just randomly come to Idlewild."

"It could happen."

The summer before my senior year of high

school, I met Adrian. His grandmother had loaned him and some of his frat brothers her house for the summer. I used to go canoeing and then swim along the lake for exercise. I miss the simplicity of life back then. Now I can see why my parents wanted me to have this life instead of the tumult we left behind in Detroit when I was born.

I remember I was backstroking along the lake when I heard a whistle. I thought maybe it was my Dad whistling out for me, but as I turned back and forth I saw a group of guys, all dressed in the same colors, all the way down to their boots. I didn't really understand why any set of guys would all dress alike when they weren't a sports team, platoon or choir. But one did stand out from the rest of them. He had a clean cut while the rest of them had that greasy hair that made curls. Again I'd pretty much only seen this on TV. My parents thought the hairstyle was ridiculous and so did most of the other boys' parents. So most of us wore the same haircuts our parents had been wearing for decades. My sister and I'd always had our hair roller set so that it stayed nice and fluffy looking, just like my mother.

Anyways, I remember just staring at them until Adrian cupped his hands over his mouth and asked me what my name was.

"Eden! What's yours?"

"Adrian!"

I smiled and then swam back to my canoe, silently praying I would get in properly and not completely embarrass myself. I started to paddle backwards from him.

"Where are you going?"

"Home!"

Yes, I just paddled all the way back home. That's your mother for you. I felt a bit of attraction to someone and I ran for the hills. When I got home I hurried into my room, grabbing for my journal. My sister, Lena turned over on her bed and asked, "whatcha writing?"

"Mind your business," I said to her.

"You may as well tell me since you know I'm going to read it anyways." Lena was the epitome *of the annoying younger sister, but she actually was my best friend. Other than your father, she still is my best friend.*

"There are new boys here."

"From where?"

"I don't know."

"What do they look like?"

"Good."

And like always my sister convinced me to do something crazy...more like something dumb. Just like the messes you and Violet get yourselves into. It was cute when I had two identical two year olds smearing lipstick all over their faces. At least I could take pictures of that. When you guys got older, it wasn't too cute.

The next day we both walked over there to get a peek at them.

"Look in the window," *Lena said to me.*

"No, you look!" *I said.* "You're taller."

"Fine, but you owe me ice cream. Black Raspberry. Two scoops." *She looked over into the window and jumped from window to window* peeking inside. "I don't see anyone, maybe they're upstairs."

"Let's just go," I said, looking back and forth around me to make sure the coast was clear.

"To Jones Ice Cream."

I rolled my eyes.

Lena and I started walking to the ice cream parlor. I always thought that Lena could be a great dancer if she was interested in it. She was 5'9, pretty much all legs. Lena had my mother's tall stature and poofy hair. I, on the hand got my father's eyes, but my mom's long lashes that had me always taking eyelashes out of my eyes.

As we walked through the door of the ice cream parlor, the bell chiming and announcing our entrance, we saw all of them there, sitting in a booth eating ice cream and laughing.

"Is that them?" Lena whispered to me.

"Shhh."

"Oh, you're right, they are cute. Too bad Mom and Dad won't let you date them," she said, laughing.

"Shut up, Lena."

I was hoping they wouldn't recognize me as I went to the counter and asked for the usual flavor, vanilla. The next thing I know, Adrian is next to me saying, "Aren't you the girl from the canoe? Eden right?" All I could think was...he remembered my name. I'm sure I stammered through my name and fumbled through introducing my sister.

Adrian had this slow way of smiling, just like the movie stars, and I could tell Lena was equally obsessed like I was. He invited us to sit with his friends and eat. They seemed so much older and wiser even though Adrian was only two years older than me. Everything they did made me feel plain, just like the vanilla ice cream I had.

Remember that time you fell in love with that boy Miles Juniper? Yeah, well Adrian was my Miles Juniper. Except, I still have no idea what would convince you to date a boy with a plant for a last name, when you already have a plant for a first name. Clover Juniper?.... Yeah, that would never work. When you started seeing Miles, I felt on

21

edge...because something felt... off. You were always the one that took after me. The dancing, our wild imaginations. With Miles, you were like me. Withdrawn, angry. It was an anger bubbling on the inside, that hadn't been released yet. Like a volcano ready to erupt. I knew just like me that one day you would burst and that anger would touch all of us, and I was scared. I was scared for you because I knew that you were too much in love with the idea of love. I wanted you to know and understand real love, not just infatuation.

I grew up enamored with the story of how my grandparents fell in love. Just like you did. But, I didn't know that it wasn't just sneaking nightly kisses and unearthing porcelain hearts that kept my grandparents together. There was the death of their mothers and a miscarriage of twins that they had to live through. They had to choose to love one another. Even when the pain from those events brought out the worst in them. It's easier to ignore those things and to settle for the fantasy that Hollywood has sold us, that it's just chemistry, cosmic connections, and even astrology signs that keep people together. That way, we can be lazy about love, we can stop choosing it everyday, and when that person stops serving our needs, we say we have irreconcilable differences.

But just like me, as much as I wanted to keep you from Miles, and you know I tried, I knew it wouldn't work. I just had to be there when it was over. I remember that in the aftermath as I held you, your tears wetting my shirt, your snot on me, yes missy, you got your snot on me, that you told me I had no idea how bad you felt. I told you that you had no idea how wrong you were.

You know, I had a life before I met your father. Hard to believe, but I did. Growing up in Idlewild was fun. Not exciting, but fun. It was fun making our own excitement like catching fireflies, only to have Lena release them when I wasn't looking.

"Fireflies have rights too," she would say.

We would weave flowers into crowns in the spring, swim during the summers, collect leaves during the fall and have merciless snow fights in the winter. In Idlewild I could feel popular because the whole town knew my name.

When Adrian came into my life, he changed everything. He and his friends came thinking that perhaps they could recreate some spring break fantasy on a lake in rural Michigan. Well, they were in for a treat, because there was barely anyone his age for miles. Everyone seemed to wait around until they were eighteen so they could leave Idlewild, the others stayed and took over their family's business or something. I was one year away from leaving for college and Lena was only 14. She had a long way to go.

Adrian went to Columbia University and I used to just sit around hearing him tell me stories about Harlem, Broadway, the Village, Soho, all these places that I had dreamed about. His father was a politician and his mother a law professor at NYU. My parents were impressed by his manners, his career goal to be a doctor, by just his presentation of himself. But, there was always an air of uncertainty with my father...and my grandfather, oh not to mention my grandmother. They all found different things about him they didn't like. For my grandmother it was the way Adrian seemed to take over. She didn't like that I let him sway my decisions. My grandfather wasn't into rich guys too much, especially people who had family members in politics. My dad, well my dad just didn't like him period. He thought he was impressive, but what did a NYC college student want with a country high schooler? Sex.

My dad would come into our room, grab a chair and talk to Lena and I.

He used a finger to push his glasses onto his face properly. "You girls know we love you, but we have rules."

"Yes, we know. No hanky-panky," Lena said.

I smirked.

"Very good, you were always a fast learner," he said, "But there's more to things than just sex."

"So no kissing either?" Lena said.

My dad shot her a shocked look.

"Just kidding," she said.

I covered my mouth to hold in my laughter.

"Yeah, you better be just kidding," he said. "I just want to leave you guys with this," he said handing us each a piece of paper.

It read, "I charge you, O daughters of Jerusalem, that ye stir not up, nor awake my love, until he please."- Song of Solomon 8:4

"I don't get it," I said.

"It means that love is a beautiful thing, but it shouldn't be awakened until the right time."

"How do you know when it's the right time?" I asked.

"How do you know spring is starting?" he said. "No one forces the season, everything just blooms on its own."

My mom was the only one who gave Adrian the benefit of the doubt. She said until she saw any red flags, she'd reserve her judgment. She reminded my father, that she'd thought he was some womanizing rich kid when she'd first met him.

At first I will tell the truth, things were wonderful with Adrian. Despite his friends being players, he seemed to be cut from a different cloth. He took me for ice cream, and I didn't order the plain vanilla anymore, but sweet flavors like orange pineapple. He wrote me letters and snuck me out of the house just so we could go on midnight walks. He was my first kiss and for the first time in my life I felt beautiful, I felt desired.

Now was he a college student pressuring a high schooler for sex? Not really. But, he did ask. At first I resisted because I felt guilty about it. Then after that, I said no because I was nervous. He would try to convince me that I would be fine, but in the end we agreed it wouldn't happen until I was ready. Even when his friends would drive out to Chicago or Detroit for the weekend to pick up girls and get away from the silence of Idlewild, he stayed to be with me. He loved me. I mean that's what I thought. That's what he told me.

When it was time for him to go back to NYC, I

felt like my life was over. No, really in my 17-year-old mind, my life was ending now that the love of my life was going to be 13 hours away. I cried for days, I wrote to him, and like he promised, he wrote back. I filled out college applications. Only applying for dance schools in NYC.

My parents weren't too happy about that.

Don't form your whole life around a boy Eden.

This boy could be in New York with another girl for all you know.

But, I wouldn't listen to them. Rebellion flowed in my veins and my father knew this. At least I didn't steal money and hitchhike across the state like him. Thankfully, they were hosting auditions for NYU in Chicago. Just like you, I was nervous. I prayed that I would keep my balance, and that I wouldn't cry if things went badly.

All the people at the auditions seemed more qualified than me, more artistic, more beautiful. I had this bad sense of self-esteem back then. Always comparing myself to someone. Usually, I always found myself lacking.

The auditions were an hour and a half class that was just technical barre work. Watching us plié, do pirouettes. When they told me that I had passed the first portion of the audition, I thought my eyes would pop out of my head. My mom screamed, just like a dance mom would. My grandma started speaking wildly in French about how I was going to have my name in lights and dance with the Rockettes. I wish you could've gotten to know your great-grandmother. She was something.

The solo portion of the audition landed me an acceptance to NYU Tisch. As soon as I got back home I called Adrian, leaving him a message that finally we would be together. I counted off the days, saved every letter he sent me. The summer before college was supposed to start, Adrian came again to see me. He didn't stay the whole summer like last time. I didn't mind because by the end of the summer I was in New York at my dorm hugging my parents and sister and saying goodbye.

"If you ever want to come to the city, my room is always available," I said to Lena.

"Yeah, tell that to your roommate," Lena said. "Take care. Tell Adrian I said hi." She leaned over and whispered in my ear. "You may be on your own now, but I'm pretty sure the 'no hanky panky' rule still stands."

I laughed.

"What are you two over there laughing about?" My dad said. "Stop hogging her Lena."

He took a deep breath. "It's not easy letting my first born go."

"I'll be back," I said.

"You better be. Every holiday."

"Every last one," I said.

My mom only came over to me and put a tiny sculpture in my hand of a dancer, her body bent like a willow tree.

"Thanks Mom."

She didn't say much, but before she left, my mom whispered in my ear, "Eden, be wise with your heart."

I did well in school. Yes, I missed home, I missed my sister, my parents, I missed the sound of the birds, leaves and crickets, instead of always hearing honking, cursing, and the squeals of the trains braking. But, I was too excited for this new world, too excited with dancing, too excited with Adrian. When I first got to New York, he took me to all the sights. In a week I'd seen Central Park, the Empire State Building, the Statue of Liberty, Times Square. Just about any tourist spot you can think of. He taught me how to use the subway system and how to catch a cab.

When I got to New York it was the first I realized that women seemed to flock to him. Why shouldn't they? He was attractive, smart, and had money. Sometimes I could sense the competition in the eyes of the other girls as I walked hand in hand with him. How they'd say,

"Oh, this is your girlfriend. Ahh, they do say opposites attract."

I liked the way he'd introduce me as his girlfriend at the college parties we went to together. He'd tell them that someday I'd be in some famous dance company. My heart would feel full in those moments. Until one of them would test me by dancing with him and grinding against him. Those nights usually ended in fights where he would call me jealous. He'd tell me I wouldn't feel so bad if maybe I started doing some of the stuff these girls were willing to do. Loosen up, he'd tell me. You're not with your mom and dad anymore.

I tried to tell him that what I did or didn't do wasn't for my parents, it was for God, it was for me. But, Clover something had happened. It was then I realized what my mother had warned me about. But it was too late. I had already made him my god. Adrian became the one I lived to make happy. His opinion mattered more than anyone else's, and because I fed on his praises, I was crushed by his criticism.

He would curse at me and tell me how I needed to do more to make him happy. He'd started cheating on me. I started to realize soon that this was his pattern. First it was something he'd do in secret, I'd find out and he'd beg for forgiveness. He bought flowers, wrote letters.

Eventually I gave him everything. To be honest, he didn't have to pressure me. It seemed to be the natural action I felt I had to take to keep him. As cliché as that sounds it's the truth. For a little while the cheating stopped, and I thought maybe my method had solved things. By this time I was entering my sophomore year and Adrian was in his senior year.

I should've noticed things were different when he started to make excuses for not coming to my dance shows. One night after performing I headed to his apartment to tell him that they were offering me a role in The Nutcracker when I saw a girl leaving his apartment.

She saw my frozen body. "You must be Eden."

Clover, I wanted to slap her. "Is this the part where you tell me it's not what it looks like?"

"No. This is the part where I tell you he's done with you."

She walked off and I walked over to Adrian's

door. My fight wasn't with her. He opened the door nonchalantly asking me how my show went as if nothing happened.

I screamed. I railed at him. And he didn't care. Why? Because he knew I'd be back once he came back around saying all the right things. I didn't think anyone would love me more than he did; it was something he always reminded me of. Relationships were about sacrifice. Problem was, I was the only one sacrificing. I was sacrificing myself.

Was our relationship loving? At times. Half of the excitement seemed to be him chasing me once more to gain back my trust. The times he would tell me that none of those girls actually mattered. But then, like a roller coaster that reaches the precipice we would always come tumbling down. Harsh words, lies, cheating became woven into the fabric of our relationship. I think by the time he started his first year of med school that there wasn't a day that went by that I didn't cry myself to sleep. It seemed to be the only way I could sleep once I'd cried until my eyes were swollen. Adrian didn't like me crying in front of him, so I had to reserve it for my bedroom. I wasn't getting solos anymore. My muscles ached, my stamina was low. When my period stopped I thought it was stress.

It was April, almost the end of my junior year. I was in my apartment with my roommate practicing a part for the upcoming final showcase when I felt a sharp pain. Like menstrual cramps. But worse. There was blood and so much pain. My roommate called the ambulance for me.

Miscarriage.

I hadn't even known I was pregnant.

And Adrian didn't come see me in the hospital. He called me. What if one if his colleagues saw him? What if his parents found out? He said I should've been taking the pill regularly. After that phone call, I never spoke to Adrian again. I wouldn't answer the door for him. I kept thinking why couldn't I have a love as great as my grandparents and parents? Was there something wrong with me?

I left New York after the semester and went back to Idlewild.

And then the volcano erupted. I lashed out when my parents asked me why I wasn't returning back to school. I stopped eating. My mom and grandma had to force feed me. My father and grandfather plotted Adrian's death. The only thing I didn't tell anyone about was the baby. That was my secret. Until I met your father.

If you want the rest of this story, visit your sister in Rhode Island. She needs you more than she lets on...and you need her. She may think I favored you because you danced like me. You were the one that seemed to inherit my traits. But your sister, she was more like your father. The man who changed my life. So how could I not love her? You see while you were turning perfectly across the rug, Violet had stopped to watch you. She followed behind you, with her arms outstretched, just in case you fell.

CLOVER

I don't think I had cried this much at my mother's funeral...and believe me, I was a running faucet then. But this...this letter made me feel things. Understand things.

She took time to do this while she was still strong. Took time to say something to me.

I sat on the coach bus huffing. I had to run all the way down 34th Street to catch the next bus leaving Manhattan to Providence. I took off my jacket as we turned on Broadway. It was April and it was starting to warm up in New York.

I didn't call Violet to tell her I was coming.

Violet wouldn't be too enthusiastic about seeing me anyway. We're twins and everything. Identical twins, but Violet and I always had our differences.

After my mother died, my sister and I only spoke to each other when we came home for holidays. Violet felt like mom loved me more, probably because we just had a lot a common. It always seemed like I was more of my mother's twin, at least as far as personalities, like and dislikes went. When we were younger, Violet worked so hard to force herself to be like Mom, to find commonalities. But, none of that ever worked. I can imagine it would be pretty exhausting to be someone else. Violet got along much better with Grove. Grove was always the peacemaker. The one that remembered all the scriptures that we'd learned in Sunday School.

When we found out that Mom was dying, Violet started drinking. It was subtle at first, just a sip here and there when we'd go out somewhere and people thought we were older because we were both around 5'9. We'd found out about Mom's sickness around Christmas and when Violet and I went back to school, she would come to NYC to visit me. I think she just didn't want to be alone. And I abandoned her. When she came, I wouldn't take breaks to be with her. I still kept going to the studio because *my* schedule was important. Eventually, she stopped coming and I didn't go to Providence either, because I was too busy.

By the time my mom was hospitalized, you could smell the alcohol on Violet's breath. She missed my mom's passing. She'd been at home, passed out. I don't know if she's ever forgiven herself for that.

I blame myself too. I yelled at her. I called her a selfish drunk. Grove and even Dad had been more understanding. Dad got rid of all the alcohol and gave her something constructive to do, make some artwork for the funeral. Grove would sleep on her floor the nights after, while she cried. He was trying to make sure she wasn't alone. And my own anger wanted to make sure she understood the consequences of her actions.

When you're in dance classes and the music is playing, your body reacting, your mind tends to run. My mind always returns to Violet. I seem to work out my issues with her while I'm on the barre or doing floorwork, or while I'm on stage in front of hundreds of people. It could be a thousand people and all of them will in someway remind me of Violet.

I remember staring out into the audience, thinking how many times Violet had been sitting somewhere there. How many times had she watched me rehearse? You would think with my mom being the trained dancer that I would want her approval, but actually each time I performed I asked Violet what she thought. Why? Because Violet was ALWAYS honest. I mean she was so honest that I hated getting into trouble with her, because I knew she'd always blow the whole thing. When Dad smelled the alcohol on her breath for the first time, she didn't even try to deny it.

When he asked her why she would do something so dumb, she just said, "It makes me not feel."

How many times had I sat there while she made jewelry? I always said it was too boring to just sit around for hours watching her torch metal and hammer it. I just wanted to see the final product. I was never very good at being patient. Now I realized, I had called her a selfish drunk, when I was a selfish person altogether.

My best moments were never on the stage on the day of the performance. My best moments were in practice when I finally achieved a move I thought I could never do. The moments I finally connected with a piece. When choreography just came to me.

I blame myself for never being fair to Violet. When my grieving had ended, I assumed hers should've too. I didn't even stick around while she made intricate jeweled wreaths for mom's funeral. I just looked at it on the day and I thought, "it's the least she could do for missing her death." I was the worst sister. I always wanted Violet to be this finished product. I didn't want to stick around to see her refined, bent and molded.

When I got off on Fountain Street, I caught a cab to the Rhode Island School of Design. I'd only come here once when we did our college tours. RISD was definitely different than NYU. At NYU you were smack dab in the middle of the Lower East Side. If it weren't for all the young people and NYU banners, you'd have no idea you were actually at a college. But here you knew you were. RISD looked like a colony.

Now, how was I going to get into this building without an ID? I smiled, duh, I'd just pretend to be Violet and get to her room. We had the same dark brown eyes and big wiry curly hair. I just had to work harder to subdue it everyday into a bun. But thankfully, today it had been out. Maybe, this identical twin thing had its benefits.

Dad had mentioned something about Nickerson Hall. I asked around and found my way there.

I walked up to the Resident Assistant at the front desk. "Hey, Violet!"

Oh God, I don't know her. "Hey!" I said, giving my best smile.

"You look so happy today. Did your boyfriend make you his muse again?"

My sister has a boyfriend. A boyfriend who makes her his muse.

"Uhh, you know he's such a sweetheart. You know, I forgot my ID in my room, can you just swipe me through?"

"Yeah, sure, go ahead."

"Thanks."

"By the way, pastels look great on you, you should wear them more often."

"Thanks. I'll remember that."

I went past the doors. Ok, now I had to figure out what floor she was on. I walked to the elevator and pressed the up button. Another girl stood next to me waiting for the elevator. Her hair was dyed a fire engine red color.

"Hey, Violet."

"Hey." Time to work some magic. "I'm not feeling too good. Actually, I'm so out of it. Had a nasty cold and took some medicine. It has me loopy. Could you help me get to my room?"

"Of course. Do you want me to call the RA for you?"

"No!" I cleared my throat. "No, I don't want all the drama."

The doors opened and we both stepped inside the elevator. "Ahh, I gotcha, same thing happened to me last Friday after I went out to this club with my girls."

"Yeah... so you know which room I'm in, right?"

"Yeah. 313, right?"

"That's it." I hope.

The elevator stopped at the third floor and I turned to her.

"Hey don't worry about it, I'll get to my room. Thanks for staying with me for a while."

"Are you sure? I mean I could wait."

"It's ok, my roommate is in there."

"Ok, feel better. Drink Gatorade, it helps with the hangover."

"Thanks for the advice."

"No problem," she said, as she disappeared behind the closing doors.

I turned and started to walk down the hallway towards Violet's room. What if she's not even here? I may have to wait hours for her to come. Worse, what if she's in there with her artsy boyfriend? Gross. Plus, Grove and Dad may kill her and him.

I took a breath and knocked. The door swung open and I stood face to face with her and all I could think of saying was, "Surprise!"

"What are you doing here?" Violet said, retreating back inside the room. She went and sat down at her desk, turning away from me.

I walked in and closed the door. "You know you could be a bit more welcoming. It was a four hour ride here."

"Welcome to my room Clover. Now why are you here? Are Dad and Grove ok?"

"Dad and Grove are ok, I guess." I sat down on the bed with the damask print in jewel tones. Grove had gotten it for her. "I actually came to see you."

She finally turned to look at me. "You came to see me?"

"We are sisters, right? Some may say we're even clones. I made it all the way up here with everyone thinking I was you."

"We're not clones."

"No, we're not. We are just two different souls, who just happen to have identical bodies."

"Are you here for the letter from Mom?"

"You read your letter from Mom?"

"Just answer my question."

"Yes," I said, and she rolled her eyes. "And no."

I took a breath and continued. "Although I want to see Mom's letter to you, and I want to let you read the letter she wrote to me, I'll let you decide what you want to do. But, I came here because I wanted to tell you how sorry I am."

"For what?" she said, her voice a mix of shock and defensiveness.

"For what I said the day Mom died. For being selfish. I've always been the *prima ballerina*. I'm sorry, I wasn't there for you. I'm sorry I didn't realize all the times you were there for me. I thought I did everything on my own, accomplished everything on my own, and I didn't. You always gave to me. You gave me some of the money you saved away so I could have these fancy foot thongs I wanted in middle school. I never said thank you for that." I realized I was crying. "The other day I was at school and this girl had on these really cool earrings and I said to her, you know my sister makes jewelry." I shook my head. "I realized I was bragging about you and I'd never even seen you make it. Cause my dance practices and recitals were more important."

I wiped at my nose. "I'm sorry, for being such a crappy sister. I'm supposed to be a great sister, we're twins."

Violet stared at me and got up and grabbed her coat. "Come on."

"Where are we going?"

"To make earrings."

VIOLET

I was 14 when I made my first ring. I'm not talking about those easy beaded or wire rings. I'm talking about silversmithing. My grandmother and I did it together. Since I was born she'd been teaching me all different types of art: finger painting, drawing, watercolors, sculptures. Every birthday, I pretty much got art materials from my grandma. Her best present was that the Dremmel tool and hammers, and the time she took to help me make my first ring out of a coin. After, she and I both started making jewelry until she passed.

I don't believe that people can take things with them after they die, but that didn't stop me from slipping a bracelet onto her hand during the viewing. It was my way of saying thank you and that she would always be with me.

I chose Rhode Island School of Design because of my grandmother. Even though she was a great artist regardless, I knew that she would've wanted to go to art school if she had the opportunity. So since I was her great protégé, I knew finding the best art school was the choice for me.

It was also easier for me to be away, than in Miami right after my Mom passed. The guilt was too heavy in Miami. My mom and Clover always seemed to be closer, probably because they were dancers and had a lot in common, so it was easier to be around my grandma a lot because we had art in common. It's not like I didn't have a relationship with my mom, I did. I remember everything about her, the way she smelled like lavender, and wore her hair in a bun seventy five percent of the time. She would always call me "*ma fleur*". My flower. I loved when she said that. I miss that.

The summer before she got sick we went to Idlewild as usual and she and I went to Grandma Addie's house to clean up. Now that both Grandma and Grandpa were gone, we had to keep up the place. We were dusting upstairs in my mom's old room.

"Lena and I used to stay up talking all night," she said.

"You still do sometimes," I said.

"Yeah, but that's on the phone. Look at our beds, she said, pointing out the twin sized beds right across from each other. We were roomies."

"Well, now you have another set of roommates and so does Aunt Lena."

"*Oui*, marriage and life."

"Do you regret it?" I said, covering my mouth and nose from the dust with a handkerchief.

She spun around to look at me. "No. Of course not." She dusted off the dresser. "Being in this room with my sister was a special time, but we have different times and seasons in our lives."

"Does this season ever get boring? Marriage, love, and kids?" I asked.

She looked at me and smiled. "What we think of as love, the stuff in movies gets old. Infatuation wears off after some time. Real love never gets old, it refreshes itself, so even though married people get old, marriage doesn't, and you, ma fluer, will never get boring."

"Was it love at first sight for you and dad?"

She smiled, "It was love before first sight."

"I don't understand how that's possible."

"I would pray about meeting someone like your dad. Wouldn't admit that to anyone because I was so cynical towards love, but at nights I would pray. So, I think I started loving your father before I even met him."

"Did you know he would be your husband when you first met him."

"No."

"But I thought-"

"I was a skeptic," she said.

"But you said you prayed."

"Yeah, remember when you prayed to get into art magnet for high school and then everyday you freaked out wondering if it was really going to happen."

"Yeah, but you told me I needed to learn how to have faith."

"Yes, I told you that because it's a lesson I had to learn," she pinched my nose. "It doesn't make a whole lot of sense now, but I'll explain it some day."

"*Promettre?*"

"*Promettre.*"

TO: VIOLET

You are the one that I've decided to share my love story with first. Why? Out of all my kids, you're the romantic. Violet, I see you. I've always seen you. You stare at the rings in the glass cases just a little while longer than Clover. You pause and watch the bridal gown commercials. Clover was obsessed with the music in the Disney movies, you just wanted to make sure that Ariel and Prince Eric and Belle and the Beast ended up together. I'm pretty sure you got into jewelry making for the rings.

Well, just like the Hallmark, Lifetime and Disney movies, I can assure you that we end up together. Even though you're a whole lot like your father, I think you may be able to see yourself in me for once, to see that you and I are not so different after all.

I spent a couple years in New York and if you don't know about what happened there by now, I'm sure your sister will soon share that information with you. Did I ever tell you that if I wasn't a dancer, I'd be a writer? I guess I'm enjoying that dream now. I always felt like your father and I's story should be novelized. So here goes...

I breathed in the crisp air as I rowed on Lake Idlewild. My head turned to look at the old Collins' home. Ever since I came back home from spending the final portion of my Bachelor's at The University of Michigan, I'd been eyeing the old Collin's home. It wasn't in complete disrepair, but it certainly needed a lot of work done. I hoped that I could get it for a reasonable price and then renovate it.

I rowed over and got out of the boat, pulling the boat to the shore. I wanted to see the inside of the house to see what I would have to deal with if I was going to repair this place. I walked up to the door and turned the knob that was badly rusting. It fell off in my hands and the door opened. Now, any normal person would've been terrified to walk into this house, but not me.

I walked inside. I brushed my hand across the dusty furniture that remained. This place was going to need to be cleaned. Thoroughly. I exhaled and put my head against the wall. Big mistake. I felt the tendrils of a spider web on my head and neck. I screamed and clawed at my head, I was screaming so loud I didn't hear footsteps coming and before I knew it, a man in a suit was standing in front of me.

"It's ok! It's just a spider web," he said, holding my flailing arms.

I stopped and breathed deeply, my face feeling hot for two reasons.

1. *This was completely embarrassing to*

be caught trespassing because I was scared of a spider web. And...

2.   *Because your father was absolutely gorgeous.*

"I..I'm sorry," I said, stammering. "For trespassing."

Your father still looks good after 23 years of marriage. But, back in 1990 your father had a nicer smile than Michael Jackson from Thriller. Even back then, he was bald. Some things never change.

"Yeah," I said, as he released my arms. "I'm going to go. Again, I'm really sorry."

I turned around to leave.

"Is there something you needed?"

It was then I realized that he was wearing a suit. I wasn't sure why anyone would be wearing a suit in this place. He was tall and muscular, I could tell he was someone that either was used to labor or spent a lot of time working out.

"No, not really. I was just being nosy. It's a small town, we always know when someone new is here."

He stared at me. "Is that something I should be afraid of?"

I laughed. "That you'll get robbed or stalked?" I shook my head. "No. That you'll have a difficult time blending in wearing a suit, yes."

He looked down at his black suit, white shirt and blue tie. "I guess I'm a bit overdressed, huh?"

"Just a bit."

"I just came straight here after a meeting. I'm Adam," he said, extending his hand to me.

He was too stiff. He oozed New York City. I just knew it, I could feel it. I could see Adrian in front of me. I looked down at his hand and then back up at him. I didn't want to shake it, but I did anyway. I made sure it was firm so that he wouldn't think I was weak. "Nice to meet you Adam. Name's Eden."

"As in the garden?"

"Yes."

"That's nice. I like it."

"Thanks it was a birthday gift," I said, as sarcastically as possible.

Evidently, my tone didn't register properly because he smiled and I nearly swooned. No seriously Violet, I felt like swooning. "So, you live around here?"

"Would I be here if I didn't?"

"Just trying to make small talk."

"Is that what they do in the city?"

Finally his smile lessened and instead he crossed his arms across his chest. "Yes. How'd you know I'm from the city?"

I laughed at him. "Come on Adam, it doesn't take a genius to figure that one out."

Your father didn't look too amused. "Let me guess, you have something against city folk?"

I didn't want to answer him so instead I changed the subject. "What're planning to do with the house?"

"That's a bit of a personal question."

I matched his stance and folded my arms across my chest. "I asked because I thought that would be better than going with my assumption."

"What's your assumption?"

"You have some grandparent, maybe great grand who owned this place and left it to you in their will." I waited for him to answer.

"Grandmother."

I knew I would be right. I'd spent all my life watching people come in and out of Idlewild. "And your plan is to clean it up and sell it off as fast as possible, so you can use the money for some business venture in Chicago, Detroit, or hmmm," I said, taking a step back and examining his suit. "Wall street."

"You got me all figured out," he said. "Now, I take it you're someone who's been born and raised here and doesn't take too kindly to foreigners or to people trying to make investments on the land."

"Bingo." I turned away from him and looked out towards the lake at my rowboat bobbing up and down. "You've got the lake, so this place is worth something." I looked back at him, my eyebrow arched. "Your grandmother ever tell you much about Idlewild?"

"Not really, she left here and moved to

Chicago when she was young. Guess she didn't have too bad of a life based on this place."

"Your grandmother is Maureen Collins."

He looked me up and down. "Yeah that was her maiden name, how'd you know that?"

I looked back at the house. "Let's just say my grandparents and your grandmother knew each other well."

"Ahh, I take it they weren't friends."

"They had their differences."

"Doesn't mean we can't get along," he said. He was flirting with me. I couldn't believe he was actually flirting me after I was so rude to him.

"Like you said before, I'm not into city folk," I said, walking away.

He called out to me. "We're not all the same, you know."

"Haven't met anyone who's proved me wrong."

"There's a first for everything."

I stopped walking.

"I'm from New York, but I'm not some Wall

Street Broker."

I walked back over, folded my arms and raised my chin. "So who are you?"

"Adam Davis, NYPD. Former NYPD."

I smiled slyly. A cop. "I asked who you were, not what you do." He leaned in and smelled me and I moved backwards instinctively, staring at him like he was crazy.

"Are those lemons I smell?"

I felt my face get hot again. "Uh... yeah, I made some lemonade and lemon bars."

"I guess someone's a bit obsessed with lemons."

"You have no idea," I said, and I couldn't help but laugh. "Anyways, this house is something special. Don't sell it." I walked away heading for my canoe, knowing that his eyes were on me.

"You paddled for a long time today," my mom said when I walked in my house.

"Yeah, I went over to the Collins home today."

"The Collins home?"

My dad chimed in "That abandoned mansion?"

"Yeah, well it's not abandoned anymore. Her grandson is there."

"Oh, sorry Eden, I guess you can't buy it now," my dad said.

"Well, who knows? He might be selling the property. You can buy it from him."

I went over and kissed my mom's cheek. "You're right! Why didn't I think of that?" I raced to the door.

"Where are you going?" Dad asked.

"To grandpa's house, remember he's chipping in." I said, winking and then leaving.

My grandparents had the greatest love story. At least in my opinion. Lena favored my parent's story, although my father told her time and time again that she better not come home pregnant and unwed.

My grandparents were best friends as kids, until my grandfather became some pretty boy in *grade school and ditched my grandma. They went to the same college, but parted ways when my grandma went to France to work as a governess. My grandfather stayed back here in Idlewild, drinking and entertaining women. World War II forced Grandma to leave France and come home. When she came home, she wasn't the awkward girl my grandfather remembered...and he fell in love with her. Now, my grandma was already in love with him, but did that mean she was going to let him get her so easily? No, my grandpa had to prove himself. He stopped drinking and womanizing; he built her the house they still live in today. His life changed when he fell in love. He grew up.*

I think every girl hopes her life can affect the man she loves in that way. She hopes that he'll lock eyes with her and his life will change...and that in turn hers will too. A love like the one my grandparents had, and even the one that my parents have, doesn't come without struggle.

I knocked on the front door and my grandma

opened the door.

"Eden!" She said, giving me a hug and kiss. I walked inside and smelled cinnamon.

"Something smells good."

"Yes, Henry decided he wanted to make cinnamon rolls."

Did I mention every woman wants a man who can cook for her?

"You're a lucky woman, Grandma."

She laughed. "Yes, I am very blessed."

My grandparents were both 74 years old. Both, looked like they didn't want to slow down even though their bodies were telling them something else.

"Do I hear my oldest grandchild in here?" I heard my grandfather say before he appeared at the steps.

"Well it ain't Lena, all the way in Chicago."

My grandfather laughed and then came down and gave me a hug. "When is Lena coming home anyways?"

"Christmas. She seems really preoccupied,

with all of her singing gigs."

"Don't be surprised if she's met someone over there in Chicago," my grandmother said.

"Yes, we want to see at least one wedding before one of us dies," my grandfather said.

"Well, you have better luck with Lena."

"It's always the one's that don't want love that seem to get hit right between the eyes with it," my grandfather said.

"Like you?"

"No, like your grandmother. She couldn't resist me." He said, poking her. She swatted at his hand and smiled.

Yeah, I didn't think I'd have anything close to what my grandparents had. It was as if they still looked at each other as the twenty something year olds that they once were.

"So, I visited the Collins' house today."

"Ahhh I see," my grandma said.

"I came to see you guys of course, but I met her grandson and I think he might be selling the place."

"So you want to make an offer?" Grandpa said.

"Yes. And I want to know if your offer to chip in is still good."

He rolled his eyes and smiled. "Of course it's still good."

I walked over to the kitchen and grabbed one of the cinnamon rolls and bit into it. "So how much?"

He chuckled. "Five."

"Five thousand!" I said, almost dropping the cinnamon roll.

"Yes, five thousand, is that too little for the prima ballerina?"

"No, that's way more than I was expecting. Thank you! Thank you!" I said, kissing his cheek. "You guys really do love me."

"I feel used," my grandfather said jokingly, wiping his cheek.

The next morning instead of taking my canoe

out to the Collins' place, I decided to jog over there. I put on a sweat suit, my Walkman, and jogged there the whole way hearing my clothes swish. I got to the house and knocked on the door. Nothing. Maybe he was out. I decided to go to the lake and wait for him.

Until I saw him in the lake...bathing. He didn't notice me as he put a towel around himself, shivering.

I grabbed onto the branch of a nearby tree and ended up making a rustling sound. He looked over and locked eyes with me. I don't think I've been quite as embarrassed in my whole life. "I can explain," I said.

"You know, you should've become a detective if you liked snooping so much."

I smirked. "I wasn't trying to snoop. I knocked on your door and you weren't there..." He was still looking at me like he was enjoying my embarrassment. "I never took you for the skinny dipping type."

"The water isn't running in the house."

69

"Ahh...I see." I looked away from him now. He was naked! I mean it wasn't as if I hadn't seen this before, but it was still making me uncomfortable. "You should go inside, you'll catch a cold."

"I would invite you in, but it's a mess, you'll probably sneeze all day." I nodded, avoiding his eyes. "Don't go anywhere I'll be right back," he said.

"I can come back later."

"No, no stay. I want to figure out why you graced me with your presence."

I scratched my head. "Ok, I'll wait."

He went inside and I took a deep breath. No, no, no, I couldn't let this guy rattle my nerves. All I needed to remember was the last guy to rattle me this way had been Adrian, and just like Adrian this guy had come from New York. Don't make the same mistake, I said to myself over and over.

I stared at the lake until I heard his footsteps behind me. "Warm now?" I asked, turning around to him.

"Yes. Much warmer."

"Summers aren't very hot out here."

"I'm learning that fast."

I smiled. "You see if you were from Chicago or Detroit, a cool summer wouldn't be too much of a surprise."

"Cut me some slack, I'm new."

"Nope, city folk don't get my sympathies," I said.

He held eye contact with me and I didn't look away. He was challenging me. "Maybe you shouldn't hang around me. Wouldn't want my city ways to rub off on you."

"There's no way they'll rub off on me. Trust me Adam-

"Davis."

"Right. Adam Davis, I don't take kindly to people who come in this community and then just sell off the property like it has no meaning. No historical significance. But, I came here to call a truce."

"A truce?"

"Yes. You sell me the house and all's well in

Idlewild."

He stared at me. I didn't like it when he stared. I felt like his dark eyes could see the parts of me I wanted to remain hidden.

"How much are you willing to give me for the house?"

"Fifty thousand."

"Is that a down payment?"

"Of course not, that's the full price."

He laughed out loud. "You're practically asking me to give you the house."

I narrowed my eyes. "No, I want you to listen to a voice of reason. It's fat chance you'll sell this house. It needs a lot of work. Fifty grand is a gift. The only people buying property up here are those invested in the history...and those people are dying off. Sure you'll find someone who will take it off your hands, but they won't be able to afford how much you'll want to ask for the place. They'll treat it poorly and the integrity of the community will be ruined."

"You really care about this old sleepy place,

huh?"

I exhaled out of frustration. "Yes, if you couldn't tell. It was where our people came when they couldn't even grace being in the Waldorf-Astoria. All the music greats came through here. It was where my grandparents grew up and fell in love. My parents came here and started a family. I grew up here."

His smirk disappeared. "I...well I understand. No, I take that back, I don't understand what that's like. But, I can tell you I'm not selling the place right now. I needed some time away from the city. And Idlewild, sure is different from Harlem."

I closed my eyes. "So you're staying?" I didn't know if I wanted him to stay. Actually, I wanted him to stay. I just didn't know if I could handle him staying. In a place like Idlewild, I wouldn't be able to avoid him for too long.

"Yeah for a while. Don't know if I'll last for long in the cold, but I'm willing to try."

"That's good. I'm sorry I assumed you were..."

I stumbled over my words. "I hope you have a good time cleaning." I started to walk off knowing that my chances of making the Collins' home mine was slim.

"So that's it? I hope you have good time cleaning?"

I turned around to face him. "What else am I supposed to say? I just attacked you for no reason. I look like an idiot."

He looked at me and then started laughing. Violet, your father laughed at me until he held his stomach. I was seeing red, I could've thrown a rock at him, but instead I rolled my eyes and walked off.

"Come on, don't do that!" he said, running over to me.

"Do what?"

"Throw a fit because you're a little embarrassed. It's ok, I don't bite."

"How would I know you don't bite? Cause you're a cop?"

He straightened up. "No, because I've given

you no reason to think of me as a bad person."

"You've given me no reason to think of you as good."

"You have a twisted way of looking at it."

I smirked and looked off. "Why are you a former NYPD?"

"Let's just say the NYPD and I had our differences."

"Just like I thought. You've still given me no reason to think of you as good."

All my life I've always been the sensitive one. Lena was the carefree one. I think that's why I made a good dancer and Lena was a good singer. I could feel everything in the music without words and Lena was carefree enough to sing her heart out.

My mom used to be so invested in releasing our creativity, the same way she had all of you finger painting by the time you guys could sit up. My mom would gather Lena and I and we'd get outside on the dock. My mom would set up her easel, Lena would just sing whatever came to her mind, I'd dance, and my mom would paint what she felt in the music.

It's funny that my dad, the logical lawyer was stuck in a house of these artsy people. He loved it though. We entertained him in the midst of reading boring legal documents. I used to ask my dad if he ever wanted a son, he would just say, "I have everything I need right now. I'll get my sons someday when my daughters marry."

Well, like I told my grandfather, I thought back then that Lena was his only hope at having a son in law.

"Was the guy selling?" My dad popped his head in my room to ask.

I scowled. "No, he's staying."

He chuckled. "Well, you can't hate the guy for that. It could be an inheritance. You wouldn't want someone taking grandma and grandpa's house from you."

I sat up on my bed. "I guess."

"There'll be more houses. You know me and your mom don't mind having you here."

"I'm 23, you really don't think its time for me to start looking for a house?"

"I didn't have a house when I was 23."

"Yeah, you had a ratty apartment in Detroit, but it was yours."

"And you'll have yours too. Don't rush this season in your life. Things won't be like this forever."

I smiled slightly. "Yeah, I guess." I looked at his hands covered in blue paint. "Painting with mom?"

"Yeah, sometimes I gotta get out of the paperwork and work on a canvas with her even though I'm no good and she knows it."

"Dad, you're pretty good."

"Years of practice."

I smiled. "I never asked this before: How did you know you really liked mom?"

"Really liked her or really loved her?"

"Deux, je suppose." Both, I guess.

"I knew I really liked her from the moment I

saw her. Quelque chose sur ces yeux." Something about those eyes. "I knew I loved her when I couldn't stay away."

I smiled. "Comme ce est romantique." How romantic.

"Now who would have you asking about love?"

"No one, Dad."

"You know it's not crime."

"I'll stick to dancing about it."

"Yeah, well when you find a dance partner, invite him over for dinner," he said, smiling and closing my door.

You always wondered why your father and I shared lemon ice cream together. Well, that's cause I decided to wage war on your father. I knew I liked him, and I didn't want to. So I put that wall up and decided to be the biggest Grinch ever. Two days after my talk with him, I walked into Jones Ice Cream and saw your father deciding what flavor to get. He smiled at me and I smiled stiffly back at him. He lifted a sample spoon with lemon ice cream to his mouth. I looked over and saw that there was only one scoop of it left and I sure wasn't going home without it.

"One lemon scoop," I said to Rachel.

Maybe he'd think it was a coincidence. I handed the cashier two dollars and walked out, the bells on the door jingling. I heard him follow me out, but I kept walking.

"So you're just going to take the last scoop like that?"

I turned around, cone in hand and smiled serenely. "I'm sorry, were you also going to get a lemon cone?"

"You knew I was going to get one, didn't you?"

I licked at the ice cream. "Actually I didn't. It's my favorite flavor. First come, first serve," I said, walking off.

"I thought country people were hospitable,"
he yelled.

"I'm not from the South," I yelled back, waving goodbye.

I was behaving completely out of character. And why? Because time does not heal all wounds. Because unforgiveness is like an infection that you refuse to treat. The wound remains infected until it kills you.

A week went by and I hadn't heard or seen Adam. I didn't go close to his home. I actually took the long way to the small dance studio in Reed City where I taught dance classes. This didn't mean that I didn't think about the new good-looking guy across the lake. Every night I mentally recited to myself that good looks weren't everything and that I'd learned my lesson the first time.

I came home one day to find my mom on the dock like old times, her easel, canvas and painting supplies around.

"Feeling inspired?" I asked, walking up behind her.

She smiled. "Something like that. Missing old times."

I sat down on the dock and shrugged off my

jacket. I opened my duffel bag and pulled out my pointe shoes. I changed out of my boots and slipped into my point shoes.

"What are you doing? You'll catch a cold with your chest out like that," my mom said complaining about my leotard.

"I'll warm up once I start dancing," I said, stretching my arms. "It'll be just like old times."

She smiled. "Should I ask your dad to come out here and sing like Lena?"

"Sure. Even though you know he can't hit those high notes."

She laughed and then yelled. "Ben! Ben Carrington! Your wife and daughter are in need of your talents."

My father came outside. "When are you two not in need of me to do something for you?"

"All the times we survive the day when you're at work," Mom said. "Sing for us, she needs something to dance to, and I need a painting."

"As if the house isn't loaded with them already."

My mom shot him a look and then he smirked before singing his favorite song, Sam Cooke's "A Change is Gonna Come," while I turned and leapt into the air. My father's voice filled the air and I bent with the soul tones. My parents told me that I was born in the midst of the Detroit '67 riot. My dad missed my birth because he'd been beaten unconscious by a cop. The words he sang meant something to him, and because of that it meant something to me. The emotion he sang with was the emotion he felt as he brought his wife and newborn to Idlewild.

He stopped singing and I stopped mid-movement and stared at him. He was looking down at Mom's canvas. She wasn't done so I could barely make out what it was.

"That's us, when we first got to Idlewild," my dad said, bending close to the canvas.

"Mhmmm hmm," Mom mumbled, still focusing on painting.

Dad kissed the crown of her head and smiled. I don't know why, but in that moment, I felt a bit like an intruder. That they shared in an experience I'd never understand. I was just about to gather my things and get ready to head inside when my dad pointed at the canvas at a pink bundle in the hands of a woman, "Look Eden, there you are."

The next day, the weather seemed to go from cool to extreme heat. I fanned myself, while my mom laughed saying, "Ahh, sweet memories of Florida!"

I walked out to Jones Ice Cream and asked Rachel for the usual lemon and moved to give her the two dollars.

"Your cone is paid for already."

"Huh?"

"Yeah, the guy that was in here yesterday, came in earlier, bought a cone, and paid for an extra one. He said that it should cover your tab. He paid me extra not to take no for an answer from you." She leaned closer. "I think he likes you."

I blushed in spite of myself. "Thanks Rachel," I said, taking the cone and leaving. I rushed over to

The Collins' home, trying not to eat the ice cream, but I was forced to lick at it as it melted.

By the time I reached his house the ice cream was almost done and Adam was outside taking his trash out.

"What did I do to deserve ice cream?"

He put on the cover on the can. "You could say thank you." He was wearing a plain white t-shirt, jeans and worker's boots.

"Thank you." I said, "Still don't know why you'd buy this for me."

"Thought you'd like it, that's all."

The ice cream was dripping again and I had to lick it to keep it from getting on my hands. "Are you trying to buy my friendship?"

"I wouldn't dare."

"Good, because I can't be bought."

"Glad that you have conviction. Noticed that about you the first time I got here. You know, when you verbally attacked me thinking I was selling away a piece of your community."

"You're never going to let me forget that are

you?"

"Nope."

I sighed. "Well, I guess I deserve that."

"Guess?"

"Ok, I deserve that."

The wind rustled the trees. He pointed towards the lake. "I saw you yesterday dancing on the dock. I wasn't being creepy or anything, your dock is just in the view."

He saw us. I suddenly felt self-conscious. "That's embarrassing."

"No, you were great. Is dancing a hobby or were you a professional or something?"

"I was in a company once. I'm a dance teacher now."

"Well, you look good enough to be on a stage in New York or something."

I wanted to say that I was in a company in New York and that my life there sucked. Instead I said, "Thanks for the compliment."

"Did you go to school for dance?"

"Yes, the University of Michigan."

"Have you ever left Michigan?"

I rolled my eyes. "Why the sudden interest in my life?"

"Nothing, I just wanted to get to know you a little better. The few seconds when you're not being so defensive, you seem like a cool person."

"I told you before Adam, that I'm not interested in city men."

"No, you told me before you didn't like city folk. But, I'm realizing you don't like city men. Horrible ex-boyfriend?"

My eyes widened. Was I that transparent? But I should've known when you have a open wound as large as mine was, that it's bound to be obvious to everyone, no matter how hard you try to hide it from everyone else.

"Thanks for the ice cream, but I'm not subjecting myself to an interrogation from someone who worked with the NYPD of all places."

I walked off.

Now, Violet I have no idea why your father

kept coming back for me, when it clearly looked like I was a hopeless cause. I wanted to look like a helpless cause. I wanted him to give up so I could fulfill my own prophecy that I was incapable of love.

But the next day, I heard a knock at the door. My mom answered and I heard his voice.

"Hi, good afternoon. I'm Adam Davis, does Eden Carrington live here?"

"Yes, she does. I'm her mother, Addie."

"Nice to meet you."

I walked up behind my mother. "Adam, what are you doing here?"

"Uhh, I just came to talk to you about yesterday."

I sighed. "Mom, I'll be back in just a moment."

My mom leaned over and whispered, "He's cute. Don't mess this up." My face got hot and I raced outside and closed the door.

"What are you doing here?" I said. "How do you know where I live?"

"Perks of being in a small town."

I wasn't amused.

"What did your mother say to you?" he asked.

"She thinks you're a potential boyfriend, but you're not."

"So, no boyfriend? I was sure that guys found your personality so charming."

I stifled a laugh. I couldn't help it.

"Whoa was that a smile? Did I actually make you smile by teasing you?"

I folded my arms. "I thought it was a clever comeback. Now, Davis why are you here?"

"I think we've gotten off on a bad foot. It's a small community, I don't want to make enemies."

I narrowed my eyes. "Why do you care whether I like you or not?"

"Well, let me be honest since I don't think beating around the bush works with you. I like you. I think if you give me an ounce of a chance, you'll see I'm not that bad."

I exhaled loudly. "You are two things I don't like...a smooth talker and a New Yorker."

"You think I'm a smooth talker?"

"Oh, I know you are. You probably had a lot of women back in New York, why don't you go back to them?"

A cool breeze was blowing, tossing my ponytail to the side. Despite the coolness, my palms were sweaty. I rubbed them on my tights.

"I'm not as bad of a guy as you think I am."

"I don't think anything of you," I said, before I could take it back. I closed my eyes and sucked in a breath. "I didn't mean-

He put up his hand. "Yes, you did. Why are you so angry?"

"Why did you leave the NYPD?"

He rested his tongue on the inside of his cheek for moment. "I asked first."

"I'm not answering until you do."

"You're something else, you know that?"

"Yup. That's what my mom always says about me." I leaned forward and whispered. "I hope she heard me." I leaned back and smiled. "Let's walk."

I led the way to the back of the house. We walked down the dock and I sat down at the edge of it and stuck my hand in the water to distract myself. Ripples formed around my hand.

"You look nice in your ballet gear," he said.

My heart jumped, but I kept my face straight. "Stop flirting with me."

"Kinda hard not to," he said, and I smiled despite trying to remain stony.

Your father was something else. To this day when he smiles, he has the ability to disarm me, no matter how mad I am. I can pretend to be mad, turn off the room lights and the darkness; I'll still turn away and smile.

"The force was doing things that went against my conscience and I had to make a choice whether to become someone I didn't want to be or to leave."

I examined him, the sun out in full force. I could see the sun on his jaw. "I'm sorry."

"Yeah, me too." He turned his face to the water. "People were hurt, by the things that happened."

"Well, I guess it's a gift from God that your

grandmother left you her house."

He smirked. "Yes, she said it was providence."

I raised my eyebrows.

"She left me a stack of letters. I'm supposed to open them at different stages."

Letters. "That's pretty nice. It doesn't seem like your grandmother."

"What does that mean?"

"Uhh, sorry, that didn't come out the right way. Well, I've always heard about your grandmother as someone that was pretty ticked at my grandparents relationship."

"Meaning that you've heard that my grandmother is horrible."

"No, not horrible. My grandma told me that they had an understanding, and that at the end of the day there were no hard feelings."

He nodded. "I'm just starting to learn things about her. She was always the nicest person. The life of the party."

I smiled. "It's hard for someone to stay the same all their lives. People change. Sometimes for the worst, and sometimes for the better."

"Well, only time will tell what happens to me," he said.

"Change is a conscious decision. I'm sure your grandmother decided she wanted to be different than the person she was when she was here."

"Do you want to change? You know, not seem like you're always sucking on lemons?"

I punched him in the shoulder and then turned back and looked at the water. "Sometimes. But then other times I want to stay this way, because it's become comfortable."

"Bitterness is a chokehold, not a hug."

I rolled my eyes. "You're a philosopher."

"Nope. I'd like to be a friend."

"Really? Something tells me you're not interested in just being my friend."

He shrugged. "Wouldn't matter. Can't get past the icy exterior until you let me. I think you're scared of admitting you kinda think I'm cute."

I nervously laughed. "I do not."

"You do too. That's why you get so angry with

me, cause you're attracted to me."

I rolled my eyes and looked away from him. "It was a guy from college."

"What?"

I turned to him. "You asked why I was so angry." I put my hand in the water again, moving it back and forth. "It was a guy from college."

He nodded.

"Look, I don't think you're a bad guy. And yes, if it boosts your ego, I think you're cute. But, I also believe that I shouldn't start anything with anyone I feel like I can't trust."

I wasn't ready yet, but your father had managed to crack the wall I had put up. You see, when a woman has been hurt by a man before, sure it wrecks her confidence in men. But, it destroys her confidence in herself to choose wisely. If she was such a poor judge of character before, what's to say she won't make another bad call? Your father hadn't given me any reason to think of him as bad, but I wasn't sure I could tell the difference between good and bad man anymore.

Don't all of them seem good at first?

"*Do you want to swim?*" *he blurted out.*

"*What?*"

"*Swim? I mean can you swim?*"

"*Yes, I can swim. But, this is very random,*" *I said laughing.*

"*Yeah, I know. But hey, isn't water a great way to melt ice?*" *he said, winking at me. And guess what Violet? I actually shocked him by jumping in.*

My parents took an immediate liking to Adam, for reasons I do not understand. I thought they'd be a little suspicious of him, considering he was from New York. Like Adrian, he had a way with people. But, it seemed that the only person comparing him to Adrian was me. Four days after our swim, I grew tired of having my parents ask me when I was going to see him again, and then my grandparents coming over to ask when I was going to see him again. So, I decided to go over to

Adam's home. I remember I had spent all morning deciding whether to wear lavender or pink. My mom came in and looked at the two blouses hanging up.

"The purple one," she said, smiling knowingly. "And wear your hair down for a change."

I put it on with some shorts and headed over to Adam's. I took a deep breath before knocking on the door. I saw him peek through the window and then open the door with a smile.

"Hi, Eden."

"Hey."

"Come in," he said, moving aside.

I stepped inside hesitantly and looked around. The cobwebs were gone and it smelled like Pine-Sol. "You cleaned up."

"Yeah, I couldn't stay in a dust castle forever."

I laughed. "It looks nice in here." I liked the way the stairs were right there on my left hand side and that I could see down the hall. The only thing I didn't like was all the dark colors and heavy drapery, but that was the statement during the 1930s and 40s.

"Nice enough to sell?"

I stuck out my tongue. "Nice try."

"I'm just messing with you. I got the water and light running. So, no more watching me skinny dip."

I laughed and shook my head. "Good." I looked past him at a picture on the wall. He turned around.

"It's my grandmother."

"She was beautiful."

"Yeah she was. Kind of gross to admit that grandma was bad."

"Same thing I said when I saw pictures of my grandfather."

He looked at me. "Have you ever asked him about them?"

"Yeah, I did once." I turned to him. "I suppose you want me to tell you what he said."

"Wouldn't mind if you did."

I shook my head. "You can ask him yourself."

He rolled his eyes. "You just always have to

make things difficult. When would I possibly even meet your grandfather to ask him about his ex?"

"This evening at dinner."

He smiled. "Are you formally inviting me to meet your family?"

"No, actually my mom is inviting you. She feels sorry for you, that you're stuck in an empty house with nothing to eat," I said, playfully nudging him.

"I cook for myself."

"Yeah, well my mother is inviting you. Half because they like you, and half to mortify me."

He smiled. "That's nice. What time should I be there?"

"Five is good."

There was silence between us. I looked around and said, "So your grandmother left you letters, did she tell you how she wanted her things organized or something?"

"No, not really. It's been more like telling me her life story. Not sure why she waited until now to tell me." I thought that was the most interesting thing I'd heard. Letters after you were already

gone.

"Maybe this was the only time she could get you to listen," I said.

For the first time I noticed that he shyly broke eye contact with me. "Maybe" he said, exhaling. "I'm not supposed to open the next one until I find something or preferably someone that makes me not regret being in Idlewild. Those were her words exactly."

"Sounds like your grandmother is trying to be a match maker from the grave."

He laughed. "I think you're right. She never liked any of my girlfriends. She thought they were shallow and dumb."

"Ahh really? I thought a guy like you would only be after brains," I teased.

"Yeah, well, I was young. I was getting things out of my system."

I rolled my eyes. "All you men are the same."

He pulled out a chair for me around the dining table and I sat. He sat on the chair next to mine.

"Is that how he was? The guy from college?"

Why did he want to talk about that? I know my face was showing how irritated I was. "Yeah, he was something like that."

"Worse?"

"Yeah, worse."

He leaned his head back against the back of the chair. "I'm twenty eight years old and I have never been in love."

"It's not all it's cracked up to be."

He chuckled. "Oh really? The subject of poetry, music, the element that starts wars, that thing that motivated God, you're telling me it's not all that it's cracked up to be?"

God? Did I really hear him mention God? I thought to myself that I better not get too excited. People mentioned God all the time and then lived as though he didn't exist. I thought for a moment. "I don't know. I think there's different degrees, or rather different types of love. So the love that's in the movies, books and music, I just don't think it's that great."

"Why because it inevitably leads to heart ache?"

"Most times, because it isn't real."

He looked intrigued. "Oh yeah, what's real love?"

I smiled faintly. "Giving...serving...two people wanting to do that for each other their whole lives. That way none of them are ever empty or dry." I cleared my throat. "Yeah, but that doesn't happen too often."

"You're way too pessimistic about love for someone who has parents and grandparents who are still together."

Did he have to remind me that I was competing with them? "I think that's the problem. I always wanted what they had. I wanted that so bad and then it fell through and I've been gun shy since." I rubbed my forehead. "Gosh, I have no idea why I told you that."

He gave me a reassuring smile. "I'm glad you did."

I didn't say anything, just played with my

hands. *"You make me uncomfortable,"* I said laughing. *"I can't tell you when's the last time that's happened to me."*

He looked at me. "Same."

I gave him a small smile. "Glad I'm not alone."

"I like that you're being honest with me. You know this is usually the time when I ask you out and you say..."

"I'll think about it."

"What?" He made a show of putting his head in his heads. "I thought we were finally here." he said, pointing two fingers at my eyes and then pointing them at his.

I laughed. "I don't want to be impulsive."

"Nope, you don't want to take a chance. You're thinking I'm going to be him. And funny thing is I don't even know what he did, besides cheat on you."

"That's all you need to know."

He shook my head. "No, but I'll settle myself on knowing that...for now."

"I lived in New York for a while," I confessed.

He definitely wasn't expecting that. "What? Why didn't you say anything?"

"I don't really like talking about that time. But I figured I might as well tell you that because someone is bound to mention it tonight."

"How long did you live there?"

"I went to NYU Tisch for three years. I transferred to the University of Michigan."

"Why'd you leave in your junior year?"

"It's too soon to tell you all of that."

"Haven't you heard that confessing to stranger is much easier? That's why people go to counselors."

"Are you a counselor?"

"Nope, but I can do what just about every counselor does. Sit here and listen. Give you a listening ear, I can even serve you by giving you a shoulder to cry on," he said smirking.

I narrowed my eyes. "If I tell you, then you have to tell me what really happened to make you leave the force." I didn't take my eyes off him. "I wasn't buying the first story. I know there's more to it."

He swallowed and then nodded. "Deal."

I got up. "Come on, let's take a walk. I prefer to walk and talk. Plus, it's a small town people will think we're in here doing things if we stay too long."

He laughed and followed me outside. I started to walk towards an opening in the trees. It was a trail through the woods that led back out to the street.

"You don't expect me to walk in there?" he asked, his eyes wide.

"Yes."

"What if there's wolves, foxes, ticks, or deer?"

"All my life I haven't seen a wolf. Foxes and deer are scared of humans. You'll survive."

He hesitated.

"Come on, stop being a baby."

We stepped inside and I started walking while he walked alongside me. I could tell he was skittish and I think that made things easier for me. The fact that I wasn't the only one shaking. "There was a guy named Adrian that came here the summer I turned 17 and I fell in love with him. He told me that we could move to New York together, and have this glamorous life, where I would dance for some big company, and he would be a doctor. He was about to start his senior year of college and I was this naïve high school senior. Even after he left he wrote to me and so I left for school in New York and things were great. I was doing well in school, getting a lot of attention from my teachers. I was starting to blossom and not be the country hick that Adrian once thought I was." I plucked a leaf off a tree.

"Something about that bothered him because he just stopped being the charming nice guy I knew that summer. He started to just say the worst things to me. One minute he was Dr. Jekyll and the next he was Hyde."

The whole time I stayed with him. Because I thought I needed him. Because I loved him." I twirled the leaf in my hand.

"I blame myself...I have been cheated on more

times than I can count and those are the times I caught him. I have tried to change myself into twenty different women to make him feel satisfied and it was never enough."

Adam cupped my face. "You shouldn't have to change to satisfy someone."

I had to tell him the rest.

"One day I just had a miscarriage. I didn't even know I was pregnant. The doctors said my body couldn't handle the pregnancy. I was stressed out. There were days I was too depressed to eat. A couple of times I even went to happy hour. My roommate had to take me to the hospital because Adrian wouldn't come with me."

Adam used his thumb to caress my face and I choked out the rest of the words. "He wouldn't even come and see me. He said it would look bad. That his colleagues and parents would find out."

I turned away from him and wiped at my wet face. "I left school and came home. Told my parents I needed to transfer to another school. They couldn't understand why. I've never told them. For all they know it was just a broken heart that made me leave New York."

I turned to look at him. He walked back over. "Is that everything?" he whispered.

I nodded.

He smiled. "It doesn't change anything."

He held my hand and I looked down at our hands intertwined. "Your turn."

He pursed his lips. "I feel like mine is worse."

I still held his hand. "Go ahead."

He let go and leaned against a tree. "I was a cop in Harlem. We have to meet quotas and I didn't like doing that."

I cocked my head and he continued. "They want us to write up a certain amount of people for the month. And so for those who can't find actual offenders, we target and harass them until we make them an offender."

He rubbed his head. "I didn't like doing it. I got in trouble, written up quite a few times for failure to comply with orders. There's was this kid, Kevin, that used to hang out close by where I was taken *off patrol for disciplinary actions. He's a good kid, and one day I saw some cops messing with him."* He looked like he was in pain just telling the story.

"Kevin got a little slick at the mouth. I warned him about that, but he was justifiably upset that he was getting stopped for no reason. Anyways, one of them grabbed his arm and he tried to shrug him off, but he ended up elbowing the cop."

Adam rubbed at his forehead. *"They took out their nightsticks and started to beat him and I... I just stood there. I was thinking about my job, I was thinking how if I got fired that I wouldn't be able to afford my rent, and I just stood there."*

"Adam..."

"Kevin ended up with 3 broken ribs, a broken nose, and tons of deep bruising. Because of me. I could've intervened and I didn't. So the next day I went into the office and I beat the crap out of the officer who beat him."

I moved towards him, but he held up his hand to stop me.

"As the judge said, I am lucky they didn't press

charges. I was relieved of my duty and I have no luck in ever working as a cop in any major city."

I walked over to him and touched his face. "It's ok to cry, you know. I won't tell anybody."

He laughed and the welled up tears came tumbling out. "I feel like I ruined that kid's life."

"Have you seen him since?"

"Yeah, I visited him in the hospital." He wiped at his face. "I actually confessed everything to him and his family. I emptied out almost everything in my savings and put it towards his college fund."

"Giving away all of that didn't make you feel better did it?"

He shook his head. "No. Not even when he came to testify at my disciplinary hearing."

"He testified at your hearing?"

"Yes, he wanted to."

I wiped at the tears that were on his face. "Well, it seems the only one that hasn't forgiven you is...you."

Adam looked at me for the longest time and my breathing got shallow. "We should keep moving," he said, and rose off the tree. I led the way further down the trail. We walked listening to the sound of the crunching leaves and sticks under our feet.

"So is it just you? Do you have any brothers or sisters?" he asked.

"Yes, one sister. Lena. She lives in Chicago."

"You miss her?"

"Like crazy. She was my partner in crime."

"Didn't know you were a criminal," he said, his eyes gleaming with amusement.

"Well, Mr. Former NYPD, you can't lock me up."

He grinned. "Citizens arrest."

I laughed. "Tell me about your family," I said. "They don't miss you?"

He gave a small smile. "Uhh...family life is different for me than it is for you."

I stopped walking and looked up at him.

"Well, you know about my grandmother. She tells me that she used to be pretty snobby when she was here. But, that's not the person I knew. I mean she was this nice Christian lady who owned her own bakery. My grandfather was a saxophonist. And my father was a preacher."

"So you're a preacher's kid?" I said. "I heard they're pretty-"

"Bad?"

"Yes."

"Well, I wasn't too bad. I was actually pretty well behaved. My sister was more of a rebel than I was. Well, anyway, my father met my mom one day at a church he was preaching at. My mom was a recovering addict, sober for years, and I think my dad was a bit of a hero to her. They fell in love. Nothing mattered more to my mom than my father. She would always brag about him to all her friends."

He cleared his throat and sniffled. "He died when I was about 16 and my sister was 13. Got shot in a failed robbery attempt...my mom couldn't handle it. She started drinking again. Before we knew it she was out there getting heroin. She's always in and out of treatment."

I swallowed. "You didn't have to tell me."

"I wanted to."

"Why?" I threw up my hands. "I'm still trying to figure out why you bought me ice cream."

"Because my father always told me I'd know someone was important when I didn't want to stay away."

Violet, I'm not sure if you've fallen in love by now. But, if you have you'll know the feeling of your heart stopping. Mine stopped because I realized it was the same thing my father said to me.

"Adam would you like to say grace?" my grandfather asked as we sat around the table.

He was testing him. I smiled at Adam before bowing my head.

"Sure," Adam said. Everyone closed the eyes and bowed their heads. But instead, I raised mine and looked across the table at him as he prayed. "Dear Lord, we thank you for this meal before us. For providing for us. I pray that you bless those

SHAIDA ESCOFFERY

who have prepared this meal and that all of us will enjoy our time together as we eat. In Jesus name, Amen."

There was a chorus of amens as I stared across at him. He looked back at me and threw me a wink before asking if someone could pass the potatoes. I smiled in spite of myself.

"How old are you Adam?" My grandma asked.

"28, ma'am."

"Oh, you don't have to call me ma'am."

I shoveled some yams unto my plate.

"What made you leave New York and come to Idlewild?" my father asked.

"I needed a change in scenery," Adam played with the food on his plate. "Actually, Mr. Carrington, I was a NYPD officer, I was kicked off the force."

There was silence around the table. "You were fired from the NYPD? For what?" My dad asked.

"A kid I knew was beaten unjustly and so I decided to be a vigilante and beat the cop up."

More silence before my dad clapped and

laughed. My grandfather yelled out, "Justice served." While my grandmother said to me, "pouvons-nous le garder?" Can we keep him?

My dad said in French to my grandmother that he wished he had Adam with him during the '67 riot.

"Vous me embarrasser!" You're embarrassing me!

Adam furrowed his eyebrows. "You speak French?"

My mother yelled over everyone. "Hello? There are people here who do not speak French."

"Amen," my grandfather mumbled.

"I didn't think what I did was something to celebrate..." Adam said.

"From one person in the legal profession to another, it's not right. One crime to fix another is not the way to achieve a peaceful society. But I think what we all applaud you for is standing up for someone who couldn't do it for themselves. That's commendable."

I gave Adam a small smile and shrugged.

After the dinner I walked Adam outside. "I think they like you."

He laughed. "Not sure why, but I'm glad."

I could still hear my family inside the house. "You're a likeable guy."

He playfully gasped. "What? You're admitting that you like me?"

"Shut up."

"You should say it French."

I laughed.

"Actually you shouldn't." He looked past me at the house. "You talking in French is too tempting and your dad and grandfather are probably watching us right now."

"My mom and grandmother too. Don't forget them."

"Yeah well, I don't think your mom and grandmother will want to kill me." He smirked. "It may seem like I say everything that comes to my mind, but I am exercising some self-control and if you speak in French again, I just may lose it."

"We wouldn't want that, would we?"

He touched my cheek. "Are you free tomorrow?"

"I teach a private lesson at noon tomorrow for an hour and a half. After that, I'm free."

"Ok, cool, I was wondering if you could teach me how to row that thing," he said, pointing at my canoe propped up against the side of the house.

"Sure. You gotta have strong arms though. You're looking a bit out of shape."

"Ahh, shot's fired! Well, you can tell me tomorrow if you think I have enough muscle for your boat ride."

I grinned.

"Goodnight, Eden," he said, and kissed me on the forehead before walking off. I opened the door of the house and saw my parents and grandparents sitting there smiling.

I shook my head. "You all are too much!"

I woke up the next morning and did my usual morning stretches, jazz splits, and over splits. I ate *some breakfast and headed out for my noon class. Jennifer was one of my gifted students. At this rate, when she reached 18, she could join any ballet company of her choosing.*

After her lesson, I tried to race home to beat Adam there. I opened the door and saw my mom and him sitting there.

"Hey, sweetie," my mom said.

"Hey," I said, looking at the both of them there....with paintbrushes. "You guys are painting?"

"Yeah, you wouldn't believe that Adam is actually pretty good at this. He's helping me paint this sculpture."

"Yeah, I think this may be my new calling," he said winking at me.

I stood there with my mouth open. My mother already had him doing art. I think her goal in life was to bring out the artist in everyone. She would always say that God was creative and everyone had creativity inside of them. Because of her, you got into jewelry making. I'm sorry that she's not here anymore with you, with us.

My mother smiled. "Any time you want to do some art, just let me know. But, I won't hold you two up from your date."

I gave my mom a death stare.

"What? That's what we called it back in my day."

Adam was enjoying this.

"I'm going to change. I'll be back." I raced up the stairs and breathed. I need to relax. I grabbed a swimsuit and changed into it, putting on a yellow button down and shorts over it. I tried the ends of the button down shirt and stared at myself in the mirror. "Hair down", I remembered, and took my hair out of its bun.

I walked downstairs. My mom was the only one there. "Oh, nice choice. You always did look good in yellow," she said, fixing my hair. "He's outside, helping take the canoe down."

I nodded.

"Détendez-Vous," she said. Relax.

"So you speak French now?"

"Ahh, I picked up some things over the years."

I smiled. "Au revoir," I said, and headed out the door. Adam was out there pulling the canoe towards the water.

"Thanks."

"No problem," he said, and then looked up at me. "Yellow. That was the color you were wearing the first time I saw you."

"You remember what color I was wearing?"

"Yeah, how could I forget?"

We paddled out in the direction of his home, well, let's put this correctly, your father knows how to paddle, but certainly not how to steer the canoe.

"You know you really suck at this," I said.

"Aren't you supposed to be a teacher?"

"I'm off duty."

He once again steered the wrong way.

"Here," I said, demonstrating with my paddle. He copied my motion and the boat started to head in the right direction. "Perfect."

"Where are we heading anyway?"

"To the side of the lake where your house is. I figure it'd be good for you to learn how to get to your house and back."

"I have no idea why it's been warm and then the day we go out on the water, the weather goes down to 62 degrees."

"Welcome to Michigan."

We were halfway there when I heard the first low rumble of thunder. "Oh, no we gotta get over there quick before it pours."

Adam looked up at the sky and started to paddle faster. Too fast... "whoa wait," I said, before the canoe got unstable, and then I felt the coolness of water and the whoosing in my ears. I could see him underwater, the canoe over us. I pushed up to the surface and saw him come up right after.

"I'm sorry," he said, swimming over to me.

I laughed. "It's ok, I wore a swimsuit just in case." I turned around and looked at the shore. We could swim it over. "Ok, grab your paddle and swim with it underneath the boat. We're going to secure it underneath the seats and then swim the boat over to the shore."

He nodded and I went under. He did the same and we were able to get the paddles secured underneath the seats. Both of us grabbed onto the seats and started to swim in the direction of his house, although we couldn't see in front of us. The sound of rain hitting the canoe filled the silence. When my feet hit sand, we both swam from underneath the canoe and faced the cold rain. We pulled the canoe onto land and then ran barefoot in the direction of his house.

When we reached the front door of his house, I was hugging myself and shivering, trying to duck under the covering to shield myself from the rain. He finally got the door open and he went to the bathroom and got me a towel.

"I'll see if I have a change of clothes for you," he said, heading up the stairs.

"Thanks."

There was a cassette on his mantle next to the

stereo. Bob Marley.

"I found these, they'll be big, but at least they're warm," he said, as he came down the stairs.

"Thank you," I said. I still had the tape in my hands. "Bob Marley fan?"

"Yeah, of course, my father loved him. My grandfather was Jamaican."

I smiled. "I'm going to get changed," I said, and scurried to the bathroom.

I looked in the mirror at myself, my hair wet and stringy. I changed out of the wet clothes and put on Adam's huge shirt and tried to drag the drawstring on his shorts as tight as I could. They were still too baggy and his shorts fell way below my knees. I heard music. Bob Marley's, "Is This Love?"

I opened the door and popped my head out, "Mr. Davis, what are you doing?"

"Trying to get you to dance with me."

"In this?" I said, coming into full view.

"What? It's not loose enough?"

I laughed. "Ok, I'm coming." I did a couple of chaine turns over to him and then caught his outstretched hand as he started to sway to the music. "I didn't know you danced," I said.

"I'm no ballerina, but I have rhythm."

"I see."

Adam started singing along with the chorus and I watched him, my breath caught. I mouthed the words, "is this love?" along with him and the next thing I knew Adam's hands were cradling my face and he kissed me.

Three weeks. That's all it took for me to fall in love with your father, three weeks. I broke the kiss and rested my forehead on his chest until the song was over.

When the music faded, Adam said, "Let me take you home."

Adam pulled up in front of my house and turned off the car.

"Let me walk you to the door," he said, moving to open the driver's side door.

"No," I said, stopping him.

"I wanna ask you something."

He closed the door. "What?"

"Back at your house...most guys would've..."

"Asked for sex?"

"Yeah, I'm trying to figure out why you didn't."

"It's not that I don't want to...just not yet. I didn't want to put you in that position."

"Does this have something to do with you being a church boy?"

He smirked. "Wasn't always squeaky clean. Look, Eden, this time I wanna do things the right way."

"With me?"

"Yes, with you. I'm with Eden, in paradise."

"What happens when Eve comes along?"

He started singing Poison by Bell Biv DeVoe and I laughed. "I'll see you later."

I walked inside my house. My mother came around the corner.

"Oh I was wondering..." she paused, "You're wearing his clothes?"

"Nothing happened."

She pursed her lips.

"We got soaked with cold rain. He loaned me some clothes. That's it."

She nodded. "Change back into your clothes before your father gets home."

"I will."

She sat down on a chair and pulled out one for me. I went and sat down. "I like Adam," she said.

I didn't say anything.

"I know you love him."

I stared at her. "It might be too soon for that."

She chuckled. "No, deep down you know. You're trying to convince yourself that it's too soon, that he could still turn on you."

"He can."

"But, he won't."

I sighed. "What makes you sure?"

"What guy tells a girl's family who he's trying to impress that he was fired from the NYPD?"

"I don't know...an honest guy."

"Exactly. He's honest. He's not just trying to be

what we want. He's being himself."

I tapped my fingers on the table. "What if I can't?"

"Can't what? Trust him?"

"Yeah."

"This is something they don't tell you. Love and trust is a choice. It's conscious. Sure, there are feelings, strong feelings. But, love is waking up and deciding to love someone when they're at their worst, when you're angry, and even when you're scared."

She put her hands over mine. "There was boy I met back in Ft. Myers when I was in my early twenties. Sold me the moon and the stars and then as soon as he got the chance, he just abandoned me and high tailed it to New York."

"You never told me this."

"It was kinda an embarrassing story for me. After he left, I just got real reckless. I said to myself that no one would play me again. I was going to be the one playing men. When I met your father, I thought he would just be another of my flings.

Have a good time and be done with him. But, I just couldn't leave him..."

"Because you got pregnant with me?"

She laughed. "No, because your father was the only guy I sat there and thought, I wish we could do this the right way. He was the only one I wanted a future with." She sighed. "Let Adrian go. If you ever want to move forward in life, you have to let him go."

I was so used to my mom's hands covered paint, plaster, charcoal, whatever material she was working with. Today it was a mixture of clay and paint.

"There are things that happened that I can't forget."

"What? The pregnancy?"

I froze.

"Yes, we know."

"We?"

"Your grandmother and I." She leaned back in her chair. "We've both been pregnant before. The moment you came here with that tiny pouch and the bleeding. We knew that wasn't just college weight and a heavy period."

"Why didn't you say anything?"

"Why didn't you?"

"I didn't know how," I breathed out. "Are you mad at me?"

My mom laughed. "Oh I was...I was real mad. I just felt that I've always let you know that you can be open with me."

"It wasn't you. It was me. I didn't want to admit that I made a mistake....pride."

"What's done is done. Your healing process could've been easier though."

"Yeah, I know. Pride is a bad thing."

"We didn't have those family devotions for nothing," my mom said.

After that conversation, I allowed myself the pleasure of loving Adam and letting him love me. We laughed as he imitated my dancing, we fought over his horrible home decorating skills, we prayed for his mother, we enjoyed the silence.

The months seemed like they were blending together before I knew it, it was the beginning of August and we lay out on a blanket.

"Would you ever move away from Idlewild again?" he asked me.

I stared up at the clouds. "Maybe, but I definitely would have to come here every summer."

He turned over. "What about Florida?"

"Florida?"

"Yes, the Sunshine State."

"What's in Florida?"

"Sun, beaches, a job..."

I turned over to face him. "You got a job offer?" Here it was, I told myself, the time when he would start looking out for himself and abandon me. I knew this day would come.

"Yeah, I have a friend who works at a school and would like me to go and teach a couple of criminal justice classes that start at the end of the month."

"Are you going?"

"That's the plan...I mean I really want to go."

He'd already planned on going before he said anything to me. "Ok, so go," I said, getting up off the blanket.

"Whoa, wait! Why do you sound so mad?"

"Nothing. I'm happy for you."

"Eden, you can't be serious. You get on my case about communication and I'm trying to communicate."

"You decided! It's done! Go to the Sunshine State without me!" I said, as I stormed away.

I had a problem. You see, when I got upset, I ran. No literally, I told my dad I was dying to visit my sister and needed to borrow his car. I went all the way to Chicago and decided I needed to stay there a few days with my sister.

"Don't you think you overreacted?"

"No!" I said, sitting up in the bed.

My sister raised her eyebrow.

"Maybe..." I said.

"You did. You gotta learn how to not

overreact, Eden."

I threw my head back. "Ugh...you're right. Adam has every right not to talk to me again. I was acting like a kid."

"So are you going to call him?" Lena asked me.

I groaned. "Do I have to right now?"

She glowered at me and then shook her head. "Why am I acting like the older one?"

"Because I need you."

The next day Lena and I made some pancakes, bacon and eggs. We sat on her couch eating.

"Do you love Adam?" my sister asked.

"Yes," I said, taking a sip of orange juice. "I do."

"Do you think you'll marry him someday?"

I breathed deeply. "I hope so." I cleared my throat. "If he still wants to marry someone like me."

"Well, running out on him was just about the dumbest thing I've seen you do, but if he dumps you after one mistake, then you two don't need to

be married anyway."

I swatted at her. "I'm going to call him," I said, reaching for the phone. I dialed his number. It rang on and on. I hung up.

"He didn't answer," I said to Lena.

Throughout the day, I kept calling but I kept getting no answer. I felt sick to my stomach.

I wanted to lie in bed all night long. Lena convinced me, no actually, she told me if I didn't get dressed now, and come with her to her singing gig, that she was going to kick me out of her apartment. She loaned me this green dress and did my makeup. We had to go there early so that my sister could practice and do a sound check.

"Don't sing any sad songs or I'll ruin all your hard work," I said to her as we were about to enter the lounge.

"Just singing a bunch of ballads."

I sighed.

"You and Adam will be fine."

I nodded and blinked trying to control the burning feeling in my eyes.

"I'll see you in a little bit," she said.

"Make sure you sang girl," I said, giving her a small smile.

"Always."

The place was empty except for a few workers and the musicians. I found a seat at an empty table and sat down as my sister started talking with the pianist.

I sat there watching my sister on stage in her long silver gown. She was beautiful. I was proud.

"Hello, is this seat taken?"

I was about to turn and tell this guy that it was when I looked up and saw Adam.

"How did you-

"The same way you did. I have a car," he said sitting down next to me.

I was so embarrassed that I avoided eye contact with him.

"You look nice," he said.

"I thought you'd be halfway to Florida by now."

"No, I thought I'd be enjoying a nice wedding around now and that maybe next week I'd be heading out to Florida with you."

"What?"

"You never let me finish explaining that day. I was going to ask you to come with me. I didn't intend on going by myself...so you can imagine my surprise when I went to your house the next day and they told me you were in Chicago."

I groaned. "Oh no..."

"'Oh no' is right. I worked really hard on all the plans too. Got your sister ready to come. She was real shocked to find you on her doorstep. We had to come up with a plan B."

"Adam, I am sooo sorry."

He didn't answer me and just looked forward at Lena singing and then gave her a hand gesture.

Lena nodded and started singing "Is this Love?"

"When I met you I knew you were a little a crazy. So I'll excuse this whole episode if you dance with me."

I laughed and he led me to the dance floor. I leaned into his shoulder and asked. "Were you serious about the wedding?"

He leaned back to look at me. "Yeah, I even decided to do it in the AME church, well your grandmother decided it should be there. 'Tradition' she said."

I smiled and shook my head. "Well, did she mention that I have yet to be proposed to?"

He sighed and shook his head. "There you go being hasty again. You see if you had let me finish the last time, I would've said that I want to start a life with you. Somewhere warmer."

I laughed again and he continued. "I love you and I want you to be my wife."

I swiped at the tears and smiled. "I'd like that," I said, and he picked me up off the ground, hugged, and kissed me.

Later on that night I laid in bed with Lena while Adam slept on the couch outside.

"I can't believe I'm engaged," I whispered.

"I can't believe how nice your ring is...and he gave us money to shop for your dress tomorrow? Does he have a friend?"

I laughed.

"You deserve it though," she said.

"No, I don't think I do. I think that's what makes it so amazing."

She was silent for a moment. "I'm assuming I'm the maid of honor."

I winced. "You know about that..."

She poked me. "Don't play games with me."

I laughed. "Of course." I turned over onto my back. "You know grandma thinks you've got some guy up here and that's why you don't come home as often."

Lena copied my move and turned onto her back too. "Grandma is a meddler."

I turned my head over to her. "Well, do you?"

She met my gaze. "Something like that."

"Tell me about him."

"He's my piano player."

"The one from tonight?"

"Yeah."

"So are you with him?"

"Not exactly," she sighed. "He's a widower. He has a daughter."

"Oh." I stared up into the darkness at the ceiling.

"Just what I thought. Mom and Dad are not going to approve."

"I didn't say anything. How'd you two meet?"

"We actually met because of his daughter. She's three."

"Really?" I said smiling and turning over on my side towards her. "Tell me everything."

"Well, you know I don't make enough money from singing to afford rent, so sometimes I gotta go out and find odd jobs. Well, I saw this ad for a babysitter in Streetersville. So, I thought to myself hey why not? I love kids and the people there are loaded."

"And that's how you met him?"

"Yeah. To be honest, I fell in love with his daughter before I fell in love with him. He seemed *like this recluse, not to mention that I didn't think white guys were into black girls."*

We both laughed until we held our stomachs.

"Does he know you love him?"

"No, he's told me he does. I believe him, but I don't think he understands what he's doing to his career and his daughter by having me around."

"Lena…"

"The neighbors stare at us."

"It's 1990, they're going to have to stop."

"Jenna's already asking if she can call me mommy. The kids at school are gonna laugh at her."

I touched my sister's face. "Listen to me. You are inferior to no one. So you tell those neighbors and those kids who may make fun of Jenna, that you are a diva."

Lena smirked. "Badder than Whitney?"

"The baddest."

We both laughed.

"This doesn't exactly fit into our long tradition of 'perfect' romances."

"Lena, as long as it's really love, it's perfect."

Our wedding day was cool and...rainy. Complete with your father in a white tux and my gigantic puffy sleeves that now I wouldn't be caught dead in (no pun intended). But hey, it was in style.

It was just my family and his. I was nervous about meeting his mother and sister and I think Adam was more nervous about his mom. He made her promise a million times not to try anything, he searched her things, and flushed her stash he found. She wasn't too happy about that.

After we said our vows and celebrated at our house, Adam just scooped me up and pulled me out into the rain and into his car. By the time we got inside the house we were already soaked.

There was a fire running and a blanket spread. "Who did this?" I asked and then I smiled. "Lena."

"So Mrs. Davis, what do you want to do now?"

I smiled. "I think you should help me get out of

this wet dress."

Now, go find Grove….Violet, wait for your
sister.

Love,

Mom

VIOLET

I put in the final touches on both of our earrings. Green and purple mixed together. Clover and Violet.

Clover picked the large manila envelope the story had come in and drew out some pictures my mom had sent of them. There was one of them at the lake, my dad's arm around my mom as she smiled. Another was a family picture of them on their wedding day.

"Doesn't Dad look like Tupac in these pictures?" Clover said.

"Huh?"

"Dad looks like Tupac minus the bandana

and nose ring."

I laughed. "You're trippin."

"No, look at him," she said, giving me the picture. I looked down at it. I had to admit, there was a resemblance, but they certainly weren't twins.

"See?" Clover said.

"There's similarities, but they're not clones."

Clover looked down at the earrings. "You're really good at this."

"Thanks."

"I'm going to make you design all my wedding jewelry. All my jewelry for my costumes."

"You're planning on paying me for all of that?"

"Excuse you?...we are family."

I smiled. "We gotta get Grove."

"How are we supposed to get all the way to Chicago?"

"Come on, we have our savings."

Clover's eye's popped open. "Exactly, they're

savings."

I folded my arms. "If there was any time to use it, it would be now."

Clover pouted.

"Stop being cheap," I said, as I dialed Gabe's number.

"Who are you calling?"

"Our ride to the airport."

Twenty minutes later I opened the door for Gabe and saw his surprised face.

"You told me about your sister, but I didn't... Wow."

My sister smiled. "Gabe, I'm over here."

He looked confused and I smiled. "Do you know who's Violet and who's Clover?"

He looked between the two of us. "Uhh gosh, you two are definitely identical."

Clover and I smiled at one another.

He pointed at me. "You're Violet."

"Are you sure?" we said.

"Yeah, I mean, the only time I've seen Violet wear pink is during Breast Cancer Awareness

Month."

I laughed and kissed his cheek. "You know me well. Gabe this is my sister. Clover, this is Gabe, my boyfriend."

Clover smiled and poked me. "Ohhhhh..." I rolled my eyes while she gave Gabe a hug. "It's nice to meet you."

"Nice to meet you too," Gabe said.

I'd met Gabe during freshman orientation. We sat next to each other and the first thing I noticed was his curly hair. I didn't really want a boyfriend in college. I always thought I would go through college and then meet someone special. I don't know why, I guess I had just ordered my life the same way my mom's and grandma's had been. None of them had met that special someone at 18. I mean I heard there was my great-grandmother, who had known my great-grandfather most of her life, but I just didn't expect to meet someone that I had so much in common with. We didn't start dating right away. We were friends for about a year, we just enjoyed each other's company. The more I spent time with him was the more I realized we wanted the same things in life.

When I found out about my mom, he was the first person I told, because I knew he'd pray for me. He was there for me. Even when I started drinking, Gabe was there for me. I knew he didn't approve, but he'd still come pick me up when I was too drunk to drive. He was there as I dealt with the guilt of not being there at my mother's bedside.

After that, I stopped drinking altogether; just the thought of it brought the bitter taste of regret. And as things stopped being hazy and blurred, I realized clearly that Gabe was the best friend I've ever had. Suddenly all that he'd done for me seemed clear, he did it because he cared about me.

When I was with Gabe, I didn't think about how much I missed my mom, or that about Clover, I didn't worry about Grove. When I was with Gabe, I felt free.

Even the airport was a little over ten minutes away, we had to get there early to catch the early flight out. Gabe was able to weave in and out of traffic and get us to the airport in a little over five minutes. "I'll be back in a few days, I just have something I need to do with my family," I said to him.

"See you soon."

"Bye, Gabe. I'm hoping to see you again," Clover said. "Oh, and don't hurt Violet, I hope she told you I'm the crazy twin. Tootles."

She closed the car door and I shook my head and mouthed sorry to him. He was laughing.

"You're so embarrassing," I said to her.

"Listen I'm being a representative of the family. I need him to know what the business is."

"Let's just go," I said, as we walked into the airport.

"Three hundred dollars," Clover said, as we boarded and sat in our seats.

"Shut up, Clover."

"Do you think Grove got his story from mom already?"

"I'm sure of it. I'm just wondering if he's ok."

"Why are you always so worried about Grove?" Clover asked.

The first time I got caught drinking, I'd told Dad that I'd paid some guy to buy it for me. But that wasn't the truth. I'd gotten it from Grove. After mom died, Grove started sneaking away little stashes of pills. Just to sleep he told me. But, I noticed after a while that he wasn't taking them to sleep. He was taking them to forget. And pills with alcohol don't just make you forget, they can make you not exist anymore.

"I mean the guy is doing a joint degree in law and divinity and you're worried about him?"

"There's things you don't know."

"What wouldn't I know?"

I rolled my eyes. "Because you do such a great job of paying attention."

Clover stared at me.

"I'm sorry, that was a low blow" I said, and rubbed my face. "Grove self-medicates," I whispered.

Clover swallowed. "With what?"

"Sleeping pills. Alcohol."

She closed her eyes and leaned back against her seat. "Why would you keep that a secret from me?"

"I don't know. I just thought you didn't need to know at the time."

"Is he still doing that?"

"I don't know. Whenever I ask, he tells me he's fine."

"This isn't what mom would've wanted."

"I don't think she *wanted* to die," I said.

"I'm not talking about that. She didn't want us to be like this *after* she died."

The pilot started telling us to prepare for take off and to fasten our seatbelts.

"Look at us, we're drinking and popping pills. You and I stopped being sisters. We barely ever get together as a family to just hang out. I feel like we avoid it because we know she's missing."

I pulled the earrings I made for us out of my pocket and handed her a pair. I started to put mine on. "Sisters?"

Clover smiled and put on hers. "Sisters."

Grove was living with Aunt Lena so he could avoid taking out extra loan money. Plus, he was living the high life being out there in a Streeterville apartment. We landed at O'Hare and jumped on the Blue Line and then switched over to the Red Line.

"Chicago is too cold," Clover said, rubbing her hands together as we walked down the street to Aunt Lena's apartment building.

The guard stopped us. "Who are you here to see?"

"Lena Pullman."

He picked up his phone to call and Clover spoke up, "Oh wait, tell her we're here to surprise our brother. So tell her not to yell out our names or anything."

I looked at Clover and she shrugged. "What? You know our aunt."

The guard eyed us and then dialed.

"Hello, Mrs. Pullman, I have....twins here to see you, they say it's a surprise for their brother." He nodded and then hung up. "You guys are good to go, eighth floor. Apartment 811"

"Thanks," we said, and headed for the elevator.

We knocked on the door and Aunt Lena opened and was just about to say our names when we held a finger to our lips.

"It's a surprise. Where's Grove?"

"In his room sleeping."

Well, it was still 9:00 am. We went up the stairs and opened Grove's room door. He was sprawled out on the bed. Clover and I looked at each other and smiled. So we did what we used to do in the old days, we jumped on his bed and said, "Good morning Grove!"

He jumped out of his sleep and then groggily

said, "What took you so long?"

GROVE

"Grove you're the oldest, be strong for your sisters."

So that's what I did. I was strong in front of them and I did what I had to do to get through the nights and the moments I was alone.

Dad told me first about mom's sickness. All of us had come home from college to visit. I had just started grad school and it was Clover and Violet's sophomore year. We were all sitting around watching reruns of *Martin* when Dad asked if I could drive with him to run an errand.

To be honest, everything seemed quite normal until he looked over at me while he was driving and said to me. "Grove, there's something important I need to tell you." He gripped the steering wheel. "Your mother has Lupus."

I'd heard of Lupus, didn't know a whole lot about it though. I did know that it wasn't deadly, or so I thought.

"Has she gotten some medicine?"

"Yes, but it's a bit more serious than that. Haven't you noticed your mom's been a little bit different lately?"

She'd forgotten my flight time. That was unlike her. And since we'd gotten here, we hadn't seen her jog or even pirouette randomly in the kitchen.

"Yes, I've noticed, but lupus is treatable."

"It is, but-"

"We'll just make sure we pray for her and she'll-"

"Grove! Listen to me."

I looked at him. My dad was always a big guy, I heard he used to be a cop, but since I was born he'd always been a professor. He went back to school when I was a kid and had gotten his master's and PhD in criminal justice. When I was a kid I would stay up with him. He would read his books for school and I would read mine, and then my mom would come out and tell me I had to go to bed. My dad and I got so used to it that I would still stay up and read alongside him. We would bounce current events and controversial topics off each other, sometimes arguing while my sisters and mom looked on with annoyance. But we secretly loved it. It was our way of relating to each other.

My dad juggled teaching classes, sometimes even going to court to be an expert witness, and never in my life had I seen my dad look that tired until that moment. Like someone had taken the light out of his eyes.

"Is mom dying?" I asked.

He swallowed and turned his attention back to the road. "The lupus is causing brain and lung damage. So far it's been mostly lung damage. The medicine is slowing the damage, but it's not stopping it."

I slowly rested my head back against the seat.

"We've been praying," Dad said. "We'll continue to pray."

"You sound like you've accepted it."

"I'm trying to help your mom work her way through what's happening."

No, I couldn't believe that he was accepting this. "You're already talking like you're sure she's gonna die!"

"She is!" Dad yelled out of frustration. "One day she is going to pass and that could be tomorrow or thirty years from now." He sniffled and sat up straighter. "Grove, I know this isn't what you wanted to hear over the holidays, but I wanted to tell you all, just in case anything happened."

I bit the inside of my mouth. "How are you going to tell Clover and Violet?"

"Your mother is going to tell them."

I felt like I was going to be sick. "They won't

handle it well."

"They're tougher than you think. But, I still want you to be strong for your sisters."

I nodded.

That night as I lay awake, I listened to my sisters soft muffled crying, I went to the bathroom, took a swig of cold medicine and slept.

I wanted to take my spring semester off so I could stay home with my parents, but Mom wouldn't hear any of that. She wanted us all to stay in school. I went back to Chicago, to Aunt Lena's house. That was a hard semester to get through. Sleeping pills helped me get some sleep in the night. But the looks of pity on my aunt's, uncle's and cousins' faces sometimes made me stay out instead of coming home. I started accepting invitations to happy hours with people from law school. Even though it was a joint divinity degree, being in seminary doesn't mean you're getting taught how to pray and trust God through rough times. You are being taught Greek or Hebrew and the history of the church. Not that those things aren't important. Just not when your mother is dying.

In February, Violet came to visit me in Chicago. I'd taken her to Millennium Park and we'd stopped in a restaurant I regularly visited to thaw out and get something to eat.

"How's school?" I asked.

"Good, I've been trying saving up to buy some jewels so I can make more high end jewelry, maybe sell it for profit."

I smiled. "Artist and business woman, you can help me pay off my loans."

She laughed. "Yeah, right."

Natalie, the waitress that usually served me whenever I came approached my table.

"Hey, Grove, getting the usual?"

"Yup."

"And for you?" Natalie said to Violet.

"I'll just get the buffalo wings and a vanilla milkshake."

"You two both order the most interesting combinations," Natalie said.

"It's a family thing, I guess," Violet said.

"Oh, you guys are family?"

"Yeah, Violet's my sister," I said.

"Nice to meet you Violet," Natalie said. "I'm going to go and get your drinks."

When she walked off, Violet smiled slyly at me. "Someone has an admirer."

I rolled my eyes.

This was the first I'd seen my sister's eyes glitter in months. "Come on, did you see the relief when she realized I was your sister?"

"You're overreacting."

"I'm not," she said, playing with the salt and pepper shakers. "So what? Do you two have a thing or have you finally found a girlfriend?"

Natalie was nice. She was in her senior year at the University of Chicago. She wanted to be a psychologist. I had to admit she was a really good listener. She encouraged me not to use alcohol to cope with my mom's sickness, but she couldn't stop me. There were times I thought about asking her out, but I was always just trying to get through school. I hadn't had time for a girlfriend since my freshman year of college. "With everything going on, a girlfriend is the last thing on my mind. "

Natalie came back and put down the milkshake in front of Violet and a tall glass of beer in front of me.

"Ok, I'll be back with your orders, let me know if you guys need anything," Natalie said. But my eyes were focused on Violet, and her eyes were focused on that glass of beer, her eyebrows furrowed with concern.

Natalie walked off.

"Is that your usual?" Violet asked.

I didn't answer at first. I tapped my finger on the table. "It's perfectly legal."

"You don't drink Grove. You never have."

I rubbed my nose nervously. "Things change. I don't explain *everything* to you."

Violet sipped from her milkshake and I took

SHAIDA ESCOFFERY

a drink from my beer. She watched me and I felt uncomfortable, even though I was trying hard not to show it. The same way I was trying hard not to show that Mom's sickness was killing me too.

"Can I have some too?" She asked abruptly.

I couldn't believe my ears. "What?" I shook my head. "No. You're only nineteen."

"I want the same thing you want."

"And what is that?"

"To find a way to cope."

I gave her a sip that day. Everyday I would tell myself it was just a sip, nothing to worry about. Some people grew up drinking a glass of wine at dinner. What was a lousy sip of beer going to do to my sister? It couldn't even get her remotely tipsy. It wasn't like I gave her tequila or vodka. I'd done it cause I understood what she said. I'd done it cause I'd rather her try it while I was there than with some dumb friends on campus.

In March we got the call that we had to hurry back home, that Mom didn't have too long. Violet got there a day before Clover and I. Clover and I met up at the hospital with Dad.

I walked into the hospital room and glanced at mom lying there unconscious. I didn't want to look at her. Not like that. I turned my attention to my dad.

"Where's Violet?"

"I left her at home. She said she would meet us here. I've been trying to call her."

Clover was by Mom's bedside bawling her eyes out, clinging to Mom for dear life. I stood at the end of the bed.

I heard it before I saw it. The dreaded long beep.

Clover started screaming, Dad lifted her off of Mom and starting trying to calm her, the nurses rushed in the chaos continued, while I just stood there numbly understanding the brief look of relief on my dad's face when he looked at the heart monitor and saw the flat line, and wondering: Where was Violet?

"I gotta go get Violet, I'll be back," I said rapidly as I headed out the door.

I sped west down Kendall Drive. When I opened the door of our house I shouted for Violet. Nothing.

I fumbled along the peach colored walls for the light switch.

"Violet!"

When I turned the corner, I realized why she didn't answer the phone calls or me. Because Violet was blacked out, our family album next to her and a nearly empty bottle of vodka.

After that, peaceful sleep became an achievement, and not just an expectation.

TO: GROVE

Grove...my firstborn. When we found out were having you, I was so excited and nervous at the same time. I mean what did I know about taking care of a baby? All I knew was that I wanted to name every child I had after something in nature. We'd be our own little garden with Adam just stuck in the middle.

When you were born I was amazed that instinctively I knew what to do. Even though my mom flew down and helped me with you, there was something coded in my DNA that showed me what to do. But, of course I made mistakes. I had to learn what to do if you got constipated and how to properly swaddle you. But, I think the biggest lesson I had to learn was not to pick you up every time you cried.

No mother likes seeing their child in pain. But no mother wants a weak child either. Can you imagine what would happen if I never allowed you to fall on your bottom when you were trying to walk? Or if I never let you back on your bike after you fell the first time? I would've crippled you.

I think that's why we have grief in life. If we were saved from it each time, I think we'd be crippled at the first instance of pain.

So Grove, for you I leave the last leg of my journey. The longest in years, but the shortest letter I will write. Instead of boring you with writing out over twenty years of marriage, I've decided to only give you the most meaningful conversations your father and I have had over the time of our marriage.

It won't be our arguments, although we both came into the marriage with our own baggage that we each had to unpack together. I had trust and control issues. Your father had a failure to communicate. And that's just a few of the problems we hud, which is why we've always encouraged you all to unload as much as you can before you get married.

I won't even share the conversations we've had with or about you kids. I want you to remember the times we had through your own memories.

Our biggest challenges in our marriage did not happen because of arguments, financial struggles, or anything like that. When we got married, we never anticipated the journey we would go on would leave us having a lot of conversations centered on grief.

<u>January 1991</u>

It was the winter right after our wedding, we were in Florida. Your father and I had both gotten settled into our new lives. I even found a job as a dance teacher at a junior college. I found out I was pregnant with you. Things were perfect.

In Idlewild, it was a bitter winter. My grandma had caught a cold and before I knew it, she was dying of pneumonia.

My grandfather never left her side so he caught it too. They died within two days of each other.

My grandma was the first one to go and I remember when I heard my grandfather had gone too, I just screamed. I don't know why, but I screamed and wailed. And your father just picked me up off of my grandfather and carried me downstairs and held me until I fell asleep. Like a baby.

The next morning when I asked him why he did that he said, "it was the only thing I could think to do."

<u>June 1992</u>

You were nine months old when your

grandmother (your father's mother) came to visit us. She loved you. Her first grandchild. I remember we took this picture of you and her. She was holding your hands while you were learning to walk. The next day she went out, an old friend came to pick her up. Adam was on edge the entire time. I think deep down he knew.

We never saw her again. She overdosed that night on heroin.

When we got the call your father just sat there on the edge of the bed, his back turned to me. I could hear his heavy breathing, I could see his tense shoulders.

I got off the bed and handed him his old boxing gloves. "The punching bag is still in the garage."

He looked at me before taking them from me.

"Go grieve. I'll wait up for you."

I listened to him for the next couple hours pounding at the bag. He asked why and I couldn't tell whether he was questioning His mother or God. I listened as he took a shower, and when he came back to bed he reached over and pulled me close and said, "thank you."

March 2002

I know you remember when your grandfather died. Prostate cancer. Your grandmother was the one that called me. I had months to mentally prepare, but my hands shook as I held the phone.

I remember I curled into a ball and cried. Adam just stayed there and rubbed circles on my back. I sat up and looked at the painting that my father once hung in his room. The Return of the Prodigal Son.

"Did it feel this way when you lost your father?" I asked.

He shook his head. "This feels worse."

"Why?"

"Because this is the second time I lost a father."

November 2009

I knew your grandma was ready to go. She

would always say she was ready to see "Jesus, Ben, and Mr. And Mrs. Carrington." At least she just went in her sleep. Just like that, she was sleeping downstairs and didn't wake up like she normally did to make you all breakfast for school. I thought she just needed some extra sleep, but when you all were off to school, I tried to wake her and she didn't budge.

After the paramedics took her I sat on the bed and just cried. Cried until my eyes couldn't let anything out anymore. Adam went outside and came back after a few minutes and tossed me some ballet shoes.

"What are these for?"

"Come on."

I followed him outside. He had my mom's easel set up with a canvas on it.

"Put on some music and dance. I'll paint."

"Adam."

He took the slippers from my hands, bent down, put them on my feet, and turned on a classical station.

"Dance."

I gave him a sour look, but complied. I felt pain. I felt raw. When the song was done, he turned the canvas around to show me just a canvas filled with shades of blue.

"Do you think she'd like it?" He asked.

Winter 2013

We realized my sickness was getting severe and he and I lay in bed, the lamp on. Neither of us said anything for a while.

"You can't leave me," he said, choking on his words.

I turned on my side to face him and touched his cheek. "I will try my hardest. But it's not up to me. I can't promise I will stay."

He touched my face. "I wonder if Adam felt like this when he was losing Eden."

"When I go, I want you to know that it's ok-"

He let go and turned to face the ceiling. "Don't start that. I won't, I'm not going to."

"Adam look at me."

He wouldn't.

"Please?"

He turned his head.

"Paradise can be found twice," I said.

"Adam never experienced paradise after he left Eden."

I cupped his face. "Not true. I'm sure Adam dreamed of Eden every night."

I wiped at his face. "What will I tell the kids?" He asked.

I rubbed my thumb across his cheek. "Tell them I love them and that life goes on."

Your father has been going to Jones Ice Cream shop everyday from 2:00-2:30 pm. Gas up the car and meet him there as soon as your sisters arrive.

GROVE

There's a lot of guilt associated with being a divinity and law student that's abusing prescription meds and alcohol. I'm breaking both a moral law and the law of the land.

Before my mom died, I never understood how people could get so sad that they'd want to kill themselves. After my mom died, I didn't understand how people survived depression.

It was like being locked up in a dark prison with no way to see the exit and each time you try, you just end up running into the wall.

I felt chest pain and I knew I didn't have a heart or lung condition. The only thing that could get me to sleep was sleep medication, allergy medicine, or cough syrup. I was pretty careful to hide it from Aunt Lena, in the same way I hid it from Dad. I only took two pills from my uncle Ralph's painkiller prescription bottle, then some allergy pills from my cousins Jenna and Jack, that way they wouldn't suspect it was missing. But, all of that was beginning to take its toll. I was having problems making it to class. Or making it through class. It's a miracle that I would even end this semester with a passing grade. I think they just assumed I was a stressed out grad student like everyone else.

Then I got that letter in the mail from Mom. I was a bit shocked by it. But after I read it, the next day I went to the counseling center at school. I was afraid a friend would see me and that people would know.

I admitted to myself that I was mad. Mad at God...and I realized as I said it, that a lightning bolt didn't come down and strike me. I could admit that I was angry with him. It was better than harboring that anger inside and killing myself slowly. Because unlike me, he could handle my anger.

Violet finished reading aloud the last sentence of the letter I had been given while Clover drove. She kept wiping at her eyes and then gripping the steering wheel. We were more than half way there and I had finished both Clover's and Violet's letters.

"Geez, Grove, you still read like a maniac." Clover licked her lips and then asked, "Are you guys ok?"

"Yes," Violet said. "Are you?"

Clover nodded.

"How do you feel?" Clover asked.

Violet didn't respond and I turned around to look at her. She was holding the paper in her hand, stifling her sob, before she let it out.

Clover looked panicked. "Vi, do you need me to pull over."

"Keep driving," I said.

"But, she's in pain," Clover said.

"It's ok. She's going to be ok." I said. "She's finally allowing herself to feel."

I checked my watch. 1:45 pm. We were on US-131 about thirty minutes away.

"We gotta pick up the pace Clover."

"Listen, I'm not getting pulled over by a trooper."

"Ok, I'll keep my eyes open for them, but you gotta go a little faster, if we want to catch him."

Violet had settled into silence.

"Hey, Vi," I said.

"Yeah," she said dryly.

"I'm sorry for that time in Chicago."

Clover looked over at me, confused. I turned around to look at Violet. She nodded. "We all make mistakes. That night was as much my mistake as it was yours."

I gave a small smile.

"How's Natalie?" she asked, smirking.

"Natalie is fine. She's going to grad school."

"Ask her out yet?"

"Wait, Grove has a girlfriend?" Clover said, "Am I the only single one in this family?"

"I don't have a girlfriend. Natalie and I are just...talking."

"Yeah, for now," Clover said.

"Whoa wait, what do you mean the only single one? Violet doesn't have a boyfriend."

Clover stared straight ahead and avoided eye contact. I turned around to look at Violet. "Do you?"

Violet looked at Clover. Clover winced. "I'm sorry, it slipped."

"Ok, what's his name?" I said.

"Grove, if you haven't noticed, Clover and I are 20 years old, we're-"

"Yeah, yeah, yeah, I didn't ask that. I asked what's his name?"

Violet rolled her eyes. "Gabe."

I looked at Clover. "How long have you known about this?"

"I found out yesterday."

"Oh, I gotta meet this guy," I said.

"He seems pretty nice," Clover said. "I mean he seems like he really cares about her. Who knows she may be like Mom and Dad," Clover said, winking.

I huffed. "Don't give her any ideas."

Violet laughed and put her hand on both of my shoulders. "Don't worry Grove. I'll wait until you're done with your degree. Then you'll be able to officiate."

I rolled my eyes as my sisters gave identical laughs.

ADAM

As soon as Eden found out her condition was getting serious, she started to write. She wanted to do for the kids what my grandmother had done for me. Give them one last memory of her when they thought that opportunity had already died. She'd worked tirelessly wanting to make sure she got down exactly what she wanted to say. Her long-term memories seemed mostly intact. Sometimes she'd switch memories and have me read things over to correct her. The sicker she got was the more she needed to take breaks while she worked.

The day she died, I was relieved. I hated

seeing her suffer, to see her working so hard to breathe or seeing her frustrated when she couldn't remember what her address was. I was shocked when I found a letter in the mailbox in our house in Idlewild.

To: Adam

Did you think I'd leave you out? I made sure that you and Lena got a chance to hear from me too. I saved your letter for the last. I'm glad that soon I will be going home. Soon I won't have to feel pain; soon you won't have to watch me being in pain anymore.

Adam...my love. I wish something I could say would be good enough. So, I'll leave you with this instead.

Inside was a tape of Bob Marley's Is This Love? I turned it on, closed my eyes, and reminisced.

I sat in Jones Ice Cream and remembered Eden. I remembered her sitting across from me here when we were in our twenties, and thirties, and forties. There were times I would think I smelled her perfume. Just a brief moment. Or times when I'd turn over in bed and throw my arm over and realize she was no longer there.

The door chimed and I saw Grove first, his tall frame blocking his two sisters. I stood up and caught him in an embrace. He had his mother's eyes, and her brown hair, unlike the twins' black hair and dark eyes.

"You guys got here on time," I said, kissing each of my daughter's cheeks.

"Yes, Grove applied the pressure."

"Good," I hadn't seen them since New Years and I don't know why I felt nervous. "Do you all want ice cream?"

"Sure."

"The usual?" I asked.

"Yeah, the usual, for me," Violet said.

"Me too," Grove said.

"Ditto," Clover said.

I smiled. We walked to the car, Grove with his Mackinaw fudge, Clover with her peppermint chip, Violet with her blue moon and me with a lemon cone.

"Dad did you get a letter from Mom too?" Grove asked.

"Yes. But, that one is just between us."

We all groaned with disappointment.

"There's one last thing she planned for you all. Well, the both of us."

THE CHILDREN OF EDEN

We each stepped into our homes and saw the pictures that hung on the walls. Pictures of each of us, pictures of mom, pictures of all of us as a family. Each house had paintings done by our grandmother.

Our great grandparents' house, the pale blue one, went to Clover. Violet got our grandparents home and Grove got our father's house. In each of our homes we found a note from our mother.

For Clover, she found hers in the dance studio that had been built upstairs, Violet found hers in the fully equipped jewelry studio, and Grove found his in the library.

The note only said one thing,

Live.

And for the first time in a year, we weren't afraid to.

ABOUT THE AUTHOR

Shaida Escoffery- Born in Brooklyn, NY, to Jamaican parents and raised in Miami, FL was the recipient of the 2013 Atlantic Coast Conference Innovation and Creativity Fellowship for her writing at the University of Miami under which she wrote and published her first novel Idle, Wild, Love. She is an alumna of the University of Miami and a Graduate Student at New York University.